GRIMMHAVEN

Secrets of the Black Forest

Also by Evan Chaika

THE STARCHARTER SERIES

BOOK I: PROTOSTAR

GRIMMHAVEN

Secrets of the Black Forest

EVAN CHAIKA

GRIMMHAVEN
Secrets of the Black Forest

Copyright © 2020, Evan Chaika.

Published by Evan Chaika, Edmonton Canada

ISBN 0-978-1-77354-242-3

For Bryana

For all the love and support

I kept in your favourite line

CHAPTER 01

"Stop fighting, Damon, you're only making it worse."

The bigger boy held Damon to the ground as the other boy began rummaging through his pocket; taking any change he found. Damon could feel his cheeks getting numb where they pressed into the muddy snow. They were at a Christmas market, just outside of the hamlet of Hornberg in Germany. It was a cold day, but clear; at least until the white sky had opened just moments ago and the snow had begun to fall. It was just as two of the boys from Damon's class had decided that he no longer needed his money. Damon disagreed.

"Got off me, Johann!" Damon cried; his hands pinned behind his back as he squirmed. The movements caused wet mud to smear over the front of his cardigan and into his black tussled hair.

Johann Werner was Damon's age, but nearly a head taller. His eyes were a piercing blue, and his hair was a mousy reddish-brown that bristled over his freckled cheeks. Those cheeks were also turning a shade of red in the cold air. Not that Damon could see that though, with his nose planted firmly in the muck. The second boy was spindly, and Damon winced as his bony fingers poked him as they prodded his pockets. Damon didn't know the boy's name, but he knew the boy's father ran a corner store near the school. *Anything he takes from me, I'll steal from the store*, he thought angrily.

"How much, Ronny?" Johann pressed his knee into the small of Damon's back and he yelped.

The fingers left his pocket as the spindly boy counted out loud the coins in his hand. "'Bout 10."

"That it? Johann seemed more confused than disappointed. "Let me count."

As soon as Johann had taken one hand off Damon's back to reach out for the coins, Damon rolled. The movement didn't have much force behind it, but it was sudden enough to knock the other boy off balance. Damon heard Johann curse as he toppled into the mud, and wasted no time scrambling to his feet. Johann rose to his knees, and he grabbed Damon by the calf. Damon put all his frustration into his left fist, and knocked Johann in the jaw. Ronny only stood there as his friend's teeth knocked sickeningly together. When Damon looked at him, he attempted to make a scary face. But Damon wasn't one to run away. Instead, he ran towards the other boy. It was Ronny who ran away, coins leaking like water from his fist as he nearly slipped over the fresh snow.

It was snowing harder now, and Damon wished his clothes weren't so wet. He was about to run after Ronny, but instead, he felt a palm plant firmly onto his back, and all of a sudden, he was reunited with the ground. When he looked up, Johann stood over him, blood dripping from the corner of his mouth. He spit, and a glob of red phlegm struck Damon in the cheek. He closed his eyes and wiped it in disgust. That was a mistake. He felt Johann's hands grip him around the neck. At first Damon thought the bigger boy meant to choke him, but instead he grasped the pendant chain around Damon's neck and pulled. The chain broke, and Damon watched as Johann ran, his pendant in hand.

Everyone at school knew that Damon had lost his mother at a young age. His father had taken a few of her orange hairs and preserved them in acrylic, turning it into a necklace. Some kids made fun of him for it, but they all knew that touching the pendant was thoroughly off-limits. And now Johann had dared to take it from him.

Johann hadn't made it far before Damon had caught up to him. Though taller, Johann was clumsier, and Damon wasn't letting him get away. Running past tables of Christmas cookies, nativity scenes, and bands of roaming carollers. Damon trailed him from one end of the market to the other. And even when they reached the end, they still kept running, until the two boys came to the edge of the forest that surrounded the town. Damon had already forgot about his 10 euros; they were nothing compared to what Johann had taken. The boy seemed to only want it because it meant so much to Damon. Damon might have made things physical, but Johann had made it personal.

Even though it was only around 6:00 PM, it was winter, and the sun had already started to descend over the trees. Johann paused at the sight of the looming cedars before him, casting long shadows back over the market. But when he turned and saw that Damon was so close behind him with no intentions of stopping, he entered the treeline.

The cat and mouse game continued over rock, ridge, log, and stump, until they came upon a half-frozen creek with no bridge in sight.

"Give up, freak!" Johann called over his shoulder. But when he saw the look in Damon's eye, he elected to give up, and lobbed the pendent downstream. Then he ran in the other direction as fast as he could, nearly tripping over his own feet. Damon didn't hesitate in his decision. Letting Johann go, he slid down the bank and into the creek. The water was clear and slow moving, even still it took Damon a good hour before his hand brushed across the pendant's smooth surface. Smiling he held it up to his chest. *Never again*, he thought. *Never again.*

With Damon's mind clear of his rage and urgency, he returned to the bank. It was only then he realized just how cold his legs were, standing in a half-frozen creek in the snow. It was dark now. A shot of panic ran through him. *Which way was home?* Damon had forgotten. He wasn't even sure if he'd returned to the same side of the creek he'd began on.

In the dying light, he searched for his, or even Johann's footprints. But the snow had covered the mud since then, and every which path was freshly covered in a layer of powdery white; untouched. He tried to listen for voices, but could hear none. Only the odd bird and perhaps the occasional squirrel. There was *one* thing, however. *That smell*, Damon thought. Something was cooking. A woodfire, or maybe even a roast. There were always roasts at the market. With a sense of relief, Damon trudged off towards the smell.

He'd had to take a few detours, but slowly he was making his way closer to the source, with the scent getting stronger with every step. Damon was hungry, more than he had realized, and the smell was of Christmas dinner. His father would already be mad at him for being late, and for not getting the sweet potatoes he was supposed to have gotten at the market. Those worries would have to come later, though. For now, he only had one goal.

A wave of relief washed over him when he saw the orange blaze of a cookfire smoldering through the trees. A deer was hogtied on a spit and the meat was crisp and brown. His mouth watered as he moved into the clearing. But as Damon drew nearer, his heart sank. He wasn't anywhere near the edge of the forest. Trees surrounded the cookfire on all sides of the clearing. Nervously, Damon looked around, until his eyes fell on the only other person by the fire. The man had his back to Damon. He was tall, and fat, and wore a red and white fur coat with the hood pulled up. His hands were covered in black furry mittens. *Santa*? Damon had never believed in Santa like the other kids. He'd always thought it was just a dumb superstition. *But there he is.*

Damon took another step into the clearing. As he did, a branch cracked beneath his feet. The man lifted his head and Damon froze, clutching his pendant to his chest. The man at the fire turned towards Damon and lowered his hood. Damon turned white as he laid eyes on what was anything *but* Santa Claus. This man had slit yellow eyes, furry black skin, and two curled white horns on his forehead. And the creature smiled at him.

✱ ✱ ✱

"Mr. Black!?"

Damon snapped out of his daydream. "Hmm?"

"They'll see you now, Mr. Black."

Damon fumbled at his things. "Sorry," he mumbled as he passed the clerk. "I was... *reminiscing*." She gave Damon an uninterested shrug as he went past.

The reception room at the recruitment office was as cold as the world was outside. Damon's right sock was still soaked though from the flooded pothole he'd accidentally dunked his foot in on the way over. With each step, it made a strange squishing suction sound that made him think of porridge. It had been raining not-stop for the past three days in London. Even living in the rainy city for the past eight years, he had never remembered it being *this* wet.

Even in the German springtime, we never got rain like this. Damon's thoughts returned to his childhood, but he was quickly brought back to the present when he realized he'd walked past the room he was supposed to go to. Retracing his footsteps, he started again; more focussed this time. *Three doors to the... left?* Damon counted as he went. Even though he'd been here before, the recruitment office had always been difficult to find. Every door looked like every other, and he practically had to guess the right one. Sheepishly, he entered, head down.

"You best look more confident if you want to be in the Navy, son."

Damon lifted his head. There was a smaller, older gentleman in uniform behind a large wooden desk writing on a notepad. Damon walked up to the desk. The man sitting behind only gave him half a glance before returning to scribbling something on the paper in from of him.

"Name." It was more of a demand than a question

Damon nervously picked at a scab on his arm. "It's Dexter."

The man put down his pen and laced his hands in from of him, giving Damon a look. "Your *full* name."

"Um," Damon stuttered. "Black?"

The man raised an eyebrow. His skin was dark, which made the scar below his right eye look white by contrast. "Are you telling me, or are you asking me?"

"Telling." Damon stood up straight. *Focus*, he told himself.

The man paused at sat back in his chair. Damon took a glance at the man's breast pocket and saw the name *E. Ramos* sewn in black letters. "Dexter Black, you say?" He went into his desk and pulled out a stack of forms. He paused. "You can sit, Mr. Black."

"Right. Of course." Damon gingerly sat himself down. The chair was old, and it was hard to find a comfortable way to position himself.

"Do you have any middle names?" Ramos asked.

Damon was never good at thinking on the spot. He shook his head. "No."

Ramos checked something on his notepad. "Have you had any previous service in Her Majesty's Royal Navy?"

"No," Damon lied. He felt a bead of sweat form on his forehead and prayed it'd go away.

"So," Ramos laced his hands in front of him on the desk. "Why have you decided to join the Navy?"

"To serve my country," Damon answered a little too quickly. That was a lie too. He'd figured it'd be the best answer. It was corny, but the recruitment officer seemed to like it. After Damon said it, Ramos gave the slightest hint of a smile.

* * *

By the end of the interview, Damon's ass had gone numb, despite his numerous attempts to help the situation. He'd told the recruitment officer all about this and that, half of which was a flat out lie. The signature Damon had practiced writing all week was crudely scrawled on dotted lines all across the papers in front of him. As he passed the pen back across the counter, the stack was already being fastened with a paperclip and filed into a drawer. Ramos stood up from his seat to grab something from a shelf behind him.

"You'll report to training next week. Do you know the address?" Damon nodded, only half paying attention. He was sore, and irritated, and the recruitment officer's voice was draining.

"When will I ship out?"

Ramos snorted. "Eager, huh? You'll ship out *if* you complete training, but even then, that won't be for at least another six months.

Damon wanted to groan. He hated training and had forgotten it had taken that long. *That's the price you pay.*

"You'll need to be back here in a few days for a short physical examination," Ramos continued. "To make sure you're ship-shape, as it were." Ramos never smiled at his own pun, and it made Damon wonder if he was even *making* a pun.

Before leaving, Damon shook the officer's hand. At the door, he turned around, intending to ask the man a question, but Ramos was already back to his paper's as if Damon wasn't even there. When Damon didn't move, he said; "Thank you, Mr. Black."

✳ ✳ ✳

Within a few days, he found himself back at the recruitment office, getting his physical examination. The physician found that his left hand had never quite healed properly. The man was old, and muttered in doctorspeak, going on and on about how Damon had fractured the metacarpals of the middle and ring finger, and that they had never been properly treated. The information went in one ear and out the other. All Damon knew was that his hand hurt when he held things in the hand, or made a fist. Not that he told the man that.

When he pressed Damon on what had happened, Damon dodged the question entirely. But he pressed further, so instead of answering, Damon electing to just show the physician that it didn't matter and that he could still use the hand just the same. There was a chin-up bar in the office, and he proved to the physician that he still had grip strength by performing a set. In truth, the exercise had sent shots of searing pain through his left wrist and up his middle and ring fingers. But Damon was able to hide the pain well enough. Initially, he had intended to lie and say he was right-handed, as an extra layer of distancing from his true identity. That proved too difficult to fake, however, as no matter how hard he tried, he could never get the hang of writing with his right hand. As well, twice he almost let his true name slip, but caught himself.

As the physician led him out from the room, he turned to Damon and pointed a pen at him.

"You look awfully familiar Mr. Black, are you sure we've never met?" The physician was gentlemanly, and gave Damon a sweet smile. Damon didn't return it.

"Positive."

He shrugged. "Perhaps a relative." He conceded.

"Maybe." Damon winced as he pulled the sleeve of his jacket over his left hand. He went slow to not flex it. *I really messed it up today.*

"Cottrell?" The physician was already calling in his next patient.

"Sir." A strapping young lad with crew-cut blonde hair and a clean-shaven face stood. As he passed Damon in the hall, he was nearly a head taller. Damon wasn't a short man, but he could already feel the jealousy coming over him.

The man pulled a paper from his uniform pocket and showed it to the physician. Damon was about to leave, but stopped when they began talking. Feinting to tie his shoe, he began to listen in.

"Sorry, Sir," Cottrell began. "I hate to ask, but I'm shipping out tomorrow, and I can't seem to read the Corporal's notes." He held up the sheet of paper to the physician "That says report to Admiral Charlie?"

"Carley." The physician corrected. "You're shipping out with Admiral Wolf Carley. Lucky you."

Damon must have missed the sarcasm in his voice. *"Carley, hey*?

It didn't take Damon much asking around the complex to find out that Carley was Admiral of the HMS Blacktooth, and that he was shipping out tomorrow from Portsmouth harbour for the North Sea. Word was that they would even be stopping off in Germany. *Perfect for me*, Damon thought. It was time to iron his old uniform.

CHAPTER 02

The cool dock air filled Damon's nose as he stood looking over the edge of the pier. The collar of his uniform was tight, so he'd unbuttoned it down to the nape of his neck. *I'll have to remember to fix that before the Admiral shows.* The HMS Blacktooth was set to sail from Portsmouth Harbour at 0700 hours. He checked his watch. *6:58, we should be boarding by now. Whoever this Admiral Carley is, he cuts things close.*

The crew was standing in a line on the pier. Damon had found himself at the butt end of the line. He wasn't sure if that had been intentional or not. Beside him was a brown-haired man, with biceps as think as Damon's neck, and with about six inches on Damon. *Bloody everyone around here is taller than me.*

"Psst," Damon hissed, trying to get the man's attention without making a scene. The muscular man furrowed his brow and looked around. When his eyes met Damon's, he mouthed the word *"what?"*

"You know this Carley guy?"

He shook his head. "No?"

"Well, do you know when he'll be here?"

"The *Admiral* will be here when *he* deems it appropriate." His tone very clearly said; *show some respect.*

Damon was about to ask another question, but before he could, the call came down from the other end of the line of "ATTENTION!"

Damon stood to attention. He was supposed to look directly forward, but couldn't help but take a peek down the line. What he saw walking towards them was an older man, probably in his mid fifty's with salt and pepper hair and windburn skin. His cheeks were lined with impressively grown sideburns and his jaw was so muscular Damon wondered if he exercised it somehow. His grey eyes pierced like polished stones, almost flickering in the light. Despite swords being retired from the navy for no more than ceremonial purposes, Damon was surprised to see a sharpened and oiled cutlass hanging from the Admiral's belt.

Each crewman saluted the Admiral as he walked by. Damon was so enamoured with the sword, that he nearly missed his cue as the Admiral passed him. Wolf Carley must have noticed, because he stopped in front of Damon. Damon winced as he was given a look up and down.

"Your buttonsh undone." The Admiral said with a lisp, as if there were too many teeth in his mouth.

"Apologies, sir." Damon mumbled as he did them up. *I can't afford a reprimand this soon.*

As they began to board, Damon did his best to avoid attention, but apparently his best wasn't good enough.

"Hey!"

No. Damon groaned to himself, having the unmistakable feeling of knowing *he* was the person who was being called to.

"Hey!" The call came again, accompanied by footsteps.

Begrudgingly, Damon turned around, and was half surprised to see the lad from the physician's office before him.

"I saw you yesterday. I didn't know you were also on this deployment."

I'm not. Damon forced a smile. "I remember you too. What was it... Carrell?

"Cottrell," he corrected. "Eric Cottrell." He reached out a hand. "I never got your name?"

Damon wondered just how many times he was going to have to lie about his identity.

By 0900 hours, the HMS Blacktooth was leaving port for the international waters in the North Sea. Damon by that time had already found his quarters and was preparing for a good long nap. He'd been up since 4:00 just getting to port, and was well ready to have some rest. But before he could, a head popped through the door.

"Recruit Black?"

Damon didn't turn around. *Not me.*

"Recruit *Black*." The voice was sharper this time and Damon remembered his alias.

SHIT! He swung around and did a clumsy salute to the olive-skinned man at the door. "Seaman Recruit Dexter Black, Sir."

"At ease. The Admiral wants all hands on deck in 10. Something about ship morale."

Damon nodded. "Ship morale. Understood." *Couldn't have waited an hour, huh?*

Damon was up on deck probably a few minutes later than he should have been. The Admiral was already addressing the others, and the officer who had called him up was standing next to him. Damon tried as best he could to sneak into the ranks near the back. He winced when he found himself shoulder-to-shoulder with the familiar burly recruit he was standing next to during boarding. The man scowled down at him.

Admiral Wolf continued; "It'sh come to my attenshon that a few of you among us are of the shupershtitious nature." He paused, looked not-so subtlety at a few of the crew, including the olive-skinned officer beside him. "You may have heard that the watersh we will be sailing through have a certain... history." He paused, odiously choosing his words carefully. "No shupershtitious behaviour will be tolerated on this ship. As that clear.

"Clear, sir." A hundred voices said in unison. Damon was one of them, but he said it more like a question than a statement. Truth be told, he didn't know what the Admiral was talking about. But still, he'd had some pretty crazy experiences before. One of which stood out in his mind in particular. He wouldn't be surprised if there was some sort of curse in these waters.

Damon turned to walk back to his quarters, when he felt a meaty hand grip him by the shoulder. The bigger man had a puzzled look on his face. "Why are you here?" he asked. Damon shook himself free.

"What do you mean. I'm here because I'm crew."

"You don't act like crew."

Damon got defensive. "Are you calling me what? A stowaway? A fraud?

The other man backed off. "No." He paused. "Who are you?"

Damon Grimm, he almost said. "Seaman Recruit Dexter Black." Who are *you*?"

The other man seemed taken aback by Damon's bluntness. "Seaman Apprentice David Brocksmith." He almost saluted Damon, but stopped himself.

All this man knows is how to follow orders. Damon thought to himself.

That night, Damon found himself on deck, rather than in his quarters. Perhaps he had napped too much during the day, or maybe it was the movement of the boat, but for whatever reason, sleep eluded him. He leaned against the railing, staring up at the stars. Out here there was no light pollution, and they were more vibrant and plentiful than he'd seen them in years. It reminded him of his childhood, back in rural Germany. He used to love looking at the stars there too. He'd always been awake far too late as a child. It had been hard to sleep since that one Christmas.

"Cigarette?"

Damon turned to see the officer he'd met earlier in his quarters.

"Sure." As the man pulled out a lighter Damon added. "I never got your name."

"Officer James Talbot," he answered, flicking the wheel.

Damon took a couple puffs, and flicked the ashes over the railing.

"Can't sleep?" asked Talbot, lighting his own cigarette.

Damon shook his head. "No."

"What accent is that?" Talbot took a puff. "Russian?"

That surprised Damon. He'd moved away from Germany to England before hitting puberty. His accent was all but gone, at least he *thought*. "German," he corrected.

"German," Talbot repeated, nodding his head and drawing out the word as if he'd known all along.

An awkward silence followed, broken only by the odd draw of a cigarette, and a breath out.

Damon fidgeted nervously. "What was that group speech that the Admiral gave about?" He asked the question sheepishly, knowing that he probably shouldn't ask.

Talbot gave him a solid look for a few seconds, as if debating on whether or not to answer. Just when Damon thought he'd get an answer, the officer said "Admiral doesn't want us talking about that," turning back out towards the water.

"Would be nice to at least know what we aren't allowed to talk about."

Talbot chuckled. "If you don't know, then you *can't* talk about it."

Damon shrugged, and tossed his butt over into the water, watching it go out in the dark below.

Call was early the next morning, and Damon had to man his position. He was set to the rear division, to make sure the boilers were running smoothly. Groggily, he arose from bed and wiped his eyes. He'd only gotten maybe three, three-and-a-half hours of sleep the night before. And Damon desperately needed more. Practically sleepwalking, he brushed his teeth, combed, dressed, and made his bunk.

When he got to the boiler room, he saw that 3 other crewmembers were already there. Damon was worried the others would chew him out like Brocksmith had, but instead they seemed less than concerned that he was late. One of the crewmen yawned, and the other two seemed to be setting up for a game of cards. One of he two seemed to take notice of Damon's gaze.

"I don't remember seeing you around training, stranger." He had the accent of a northerner, but Damon could recognize the slight German drawl, similar to his parents.

"Dexter," Damon outstretched his hand.

"Fritz." He took Damon's hand and shook it. Fritz had a moustache like that of a carny strongman, and Damon had to hold in a giggle. "That's Roger," he pointed to the other man on the floor. "And that's Kent," motioning to the younger man with shaggy black hair half asleep leaning on a pipe.

"I thought crew needed a *crew*cut." He motioned to the man's hair.

Kent shrugged. "The Admiral runs a tight ship when it comes to getting our jobs done, but he could care less about our appearances. Besides, what can he do now, through me overboard?"

Damon shrugged. "What are we supposed to do in here right now, anyway?" He took a look around as if he knew what was going on. "Everything looks fine to me."

"For now," Fritz admitted, cutting the deck. "But every day these pipes need to be checked." He held the cards out in front of him. "You play?" Damon nodded. "Good." Fritz smiled at him.

The four men sat crossed-legged on the floor of the boiler room playing poker for the next few hours. At first it was an innocent game, but before long the gambling had started. It was Roger who had the idea. Fritz seemed to go along, but Kent was reluctant. So was Damon, for that matter. He had very little money as it was, but impulse control had never been his strong suit. By the time their shift was over, Damon calculated himself out around eight hundred dollars. Kent was down three hundred, and the others were about even in their winnings.

"Better luck next time, Mr. Black." Fritz rose to his feet. Damon didn't move, annoyed at himself and mad at the others. Fritz must have seen the look.

"Don't be a sore loser, Dexter." He pulled around a hundred dollars from his uniform and handed it back to Damon. That's when Damon saw a bulge in Fritz' right sleeve.

He cheated! Damon realized suddenly. Instead of taking the money, Damon rose to his feet and knocked Fritz to the ground. Kent and Roger looked on in horror as Damon straddled the man and pulled up the sleeve. Damon felt a rush of embarrassment as he saw a large watch around Fritz' wrist.

Motherfuc– the punch came so suddenly, Damon saw stars. Roger grabbed him from behind and wrestled Damon's hands behind his back.

"What the hell is wrong with you!?" Roger yelled. He looked at Kent. "Go get the Admiral!"

Within 24 hours of boarding the Blacktooth, Damon already found himself inside the Admiral's quarters, looking at a dishonourable discharge for a navy he wasn't even a part of. *Wouldn't be my first, either,* he thought. Fritz was standing beside him, chewing his tongue and looking more annoyed than anything.

Admiral Wolf was sitting in his chair, staring Damon down. He hadn't yet said a word, although he certainly looked as though he wanted to. The thought of Kent mentioning getting thrown overboard made his stomach knot for a moment. But he knew it would never happen. His eyes darted around the room, just waiting for the Admiral to say *something*. The room was on one of the lower decks, on the port side, with a large porthole that let in light. Most of the space was taken up by a large oak table centring the room. Damon saw cabinet in the back filled with candlesticks, cutlery, and other things probably too fancy to be on a ship. *The Admiral likes shiny things.*

Damon looked back at Wolf. The Admiral was grinding his teeth and looking pensive. Damon was about to say something, but that was right when Wolf spoke.

"Kitchen duty." It was only two words, but Damon understood not to ask clarification.

He saluted as the Admiral waved him out.

Once in the hall and out of earshot from the Admiral's quarters, Fritz pinned Damon up against the wall.

"Just what the hell was that, huh? You think I was trying to squeeze you?" Damon shrugged. Fritz let go and shook his head. "I best not see you again, Black." He walked off around a corner. Damon brushed himself off. *Kitchen duty.* He winced. *Their loss more than mine.* Damon didn't know how to cook, but at least he could maybe filch some extra food here and there.

It didn't take long for Damon to realize how boring a prep chef could be. Three shifts of chopping this and mincing that and he was already fantasizing about leaping over the side.

"Dexter!" called the head chef. Damon looked up, with half a mind to correct him. "Bring me those peppers."

Damon moved as fast as he could. No point angering him further. But he came back, the head chef was already yelling at someone else and had seemed to forget about Damon. *Figures.* Absentmindedly, Damon began nibbling on the end of one of the peppers, too little too late in realizing it was a very *hot* pepper. Damon did not do good with hot food. Feeling that distinct feeling in his stomach, he ran to the nearest railing and heaved over the side. Wiping his mouth, he stood back up straight. He was so sick, the water looked green. *Or is it actually green?* Damon looked out over the empty sea where green fog swept over the otherwise clear water.

"Dexter!" The head chef came out after him. But stopped in the doorway when he saw the same thing Damon was seeing. And the thing was moving towards them.

CHAPTER 03

Damon, frozen in fear, stared out over the waters to where a translucent green ship swept in through the fog. Behind him, he could hear the clatter of pans as the head chef feinted and hit the deck like a sack of potatoes. Damon heard another crewman scream, and then two shots rang out over the water. The sound of gunfire seemed to raise even more onlookers to the deck.

Damon retreated back into the kitchens, hopping unceremoniously over the head chef's unconscious body. Flashbacks to his childhood were abound in his mind. Damon swung around a corner, knowing they kept the on-ship armoury right next to the kitchen storage. One of the other crewmen had already unlocked it and was rushing back up to the deck. Damon took a quick scan around. There were standard navel issue pistols, shotguns, and rifles. He even saw a harpoon gun propped up against the wall, which Damon nearly grabbed before deciding against it.

He took a rifle from off a rack, and then a pistol for good measure. The rifle he slung onto his back and the pistol he stuffed into his apron, which he only now realized he still had on. The thought of hunkering down somewhere never even crossed his mind. Damon never ran from anything, not ever in his life. So, he returned to deck, ready and waiting for whatever was to come.

Damon moved up to the railing while the deafening sound of the Blacktooth's mounted guns firing off towards the ghostly ship filled his ears. The shells struck the queerly green wood, but could not pierce the hull, only merely phasing through as if nothing were even there. Damon could hardly believe his eyes. He saw Fritz standing some distance down the deck, firing his shotgun pointlessly in the general direction of the oncoming ship. Fritz' hands shook, and even if the bullets *could* do anything, he figured the man would still be missing his target. Damon felt a clap on his shoulder and nearly pissed himself. Luckily, as he spun around, he found it was only Officer Talbot.

"Dexter!" the officer yelled, even though Damon was standing right there. "You're seeing this too, right?"

Damon nodded. "So, can we talk about this *now*?"

Talbot was unamused. "I knew this voyage was a bad idea." Damon wasn't sure if he was talking to him or himself. The officer's eyes widened. "Brace yourself!"

Suddenly, the deck beneath Damon's feet shook as the green ship rammed into the Blacktooth. But instead of colliding, the two ships seemed to *merge* into one another, sharing the same space. Damon watched as the deck crossing between the two ships seemed to warp together as the ghostly ship passed. His blood went cold when he locked eyes with what looked like a person on the other ship.

The ghostly figure was just as green and translucent as his ship, complete with a tattered green overcoat and a beard of grimy green hair. He grinned at Damon as he simply *stepped* from the deck of his ship to that of the Blacktooth.

Officer Talbot stepped out in front of Damon, raised his pistol, aimed, and then fired two rounds at the man. The bullets each found their mark in the center of his forehead, but did nothing more than go through the ghostly flesh. And then the ghost *smiled*. Talbot lowered his weapon, gobsmacked. That's when Damon heard the Admiral arrive on deck.

"What in the bloody hell ish going on here?"

Damon could see that his cutlass was in hand and Wolf was striding towards the ghost as if he was no more that a mere trespasser. By this time, the green ship had moved completely through the

Blacktooth and was sailing out the other side, leaving nothing behind but the ghostly figure and an eerie haze. Enough crew had joined them on deck for the man to be surrounded, but somehow that didn't make Damon feel any better. Nervously, he unslung the assault rifle from his back and pointed it at the ghost, joining his muzzle to half a hundred others.

Wolf made his way across the deck, coming closer than the rest. The Admiral clenched his big jaw and gripped his cutlass in a black leather gloved hand, giving the intruder a stare down that would make any living man cower. But Damon had a feeling that this was no living man.

As if on cue, the ghost drew his own sword, glowing and green like the rest of him, Damon couldn't tell if it was made of steel or fog. He pointed the tip to Admiral Wolf, but then shifted it over to...

Me? Damon could hardly believe it. He shifted the butt of his rifle again his shoulder. Damon wanted to take the shot; but Talbot had already tried that to no avail. Besides, he could see other crewmen standing behind the figure, and Damon knew that he'd only be hitting them. But beside him, Talbot had no such concerns. Either he didn't realize what could happen, or was too scared to have thought of it. He took another shot at the ghost.

"No-" Damon tried to tell him, but it was too late. The bullet cut through the ghostly figure in the heart, kept going, and struck a crewman in the leg. Frowning, the figure looked down at where the bullet had gone through, as if he expected to see something. *Or maybe just to taunt our efforts*. The injured man yelled and fell to the deck. Only then did Talbot realize what had happened. Looking sickly, he lowered his firearm.

The ghost, on the other hand, gave Talbot a look as if to say: *I already gave you your one chance*. In one swift motion, it drew a flint-knock pistol from its holster and fired it at Talbot. The Officer's lead bullets couldn't strike the ghost; but his green ones *could* strike flesh. The projectile hit James Talbot between the eyes, and he sunk to his knees. As his body crumpled in a pile, Damon notice there was no blood coming from the wound. *I'm going to be sick again.*

When he returned his gaze to the ghost, he nearly *was* sick again, seeing that the cutlass was once again pointed towards his chest. *Why me*?! he wanted to scream. All he could think was that it has something to do with that Christmas night in the forest so long ago.

Damon saw Eric Cottrell standing nervously off to one side. He had no real weapon, only a bit of pipe he must have found lying around. Still, he had it raised as though it'd do anything.

"What do you want?" he called out. "Who are you?"

"It's the curse, Eric!" someone else answered.

Eric ignored him. "What are you?" He didn't take his eyes from the ghostly figure. He was getting visibly anxious. "Answer me!"

The ghost turned. "Stay. Away." It was almost a whisper.

No one moved, until Admiral Wolf turned to his men and called out: "You've all heard the tales. You all know what needsh to be done; the Dutchman needsh a shacrifice."

Dutchman? Damon was confused. *Like the old wives' tale*?

The ghost nodded, and motioned back at Damon. The pit of his stomach dropped and he froze.

Admiral Wolf looked to Damon and turned up is nose, "I knew from the moment I met you I shmelled shomething funny about you."

What does he mean? Damon was even more confused, but didn't have time to think about it. Multiple members of the crew were moving in on him. He pointed the muzzle of his rifle at a few of them, but couldn't bear to pull the trigger. Instead, he struck the closest crewman in the nose with the butt, and then did something he decided to never do. He ran.

Is this a dream? He thought to himself as he darted from corridor to corridor on the ship's lower levels. When he was a good distance in front of his pursuers, he made a sharp turn into one of the kitchen's storage rooms and locked the door behind him. With sweaty palms, he raised the muzzle of his gun towards the door, waiting to hear a noise from the other side. Instead, he heard a noise from inside the room. Pivoting on his foot, he found Kent, curled up in the fetal position in the corner. Once the younger man saw Damon he started to cry. Loudly. Tears streamed down his face and into his scraggly black beard. Damon almost felt sorry about what he was about to do.

With one sharp hit to the temple, Kent was out cold. *If I knew you could be quiet, I wouldn't have had to do that.* He froze as he heard footsteps pass by the door. Damon held his breath as he waited for someone to try the lock, but no one did. *Why did I have to choose this ship?* He had assumed the journey would be easy, and that he'd just have been able to just slip out at one of the stops along the way. *I was supposed to be relaxing on a beach somewhere by now.*

An arm was suddenly before him, and the elbow smacked Damon across the back, causing him to lose his footing and crash to the ground, rifle spiralling away down the deck. "Are you done running, Mishter Black?" Asked the Admiral.

Damon spat. "My name is *Damon Grimm.*"

A hint of a grin crossed Wolf's lips. "That would explain it."

Explain what? He wanted to ask, but before he could, Wolf was already yelling to the crew.

"Sheaman Brocksmith!" Admiral Wolf ordered. "Sheize him!"

Damon, still dazed, felt two meaty hands grip him by the shoulders and haul him to his feet. Brocksmith led him to the edge of the ship. As they went, he could see the Dutchman cackling from where he stood. The rest of the crew had retreated a good distance away from him. *Why me?* He asked himself again. Damon tried to jerk himself free, he thought at very least he'd have the strength for that. He was able to pry himself free of one of Brocksmith's hands, but no sooner than he did, he felt a gloved hand grab him surprisingly hard by the throat. Face to face with the Admiral, Damon could smell his breath. It was like a dead animal.

"Mint?" he asked, through swollen lips.

Wolf scowled at him, the eerie green fog casting strange patterns on his features. Damon felt himself being pushed by the two men to the edge of the ship. The water lurched the Blacktooth sideways, and Damon fell hard on his knee, closing his eyes and gritting his teeth at the pain. When he opened them again, his heart skipped a beat as he looked directly down into the turbulent water, inches from the ledge. He tried to crawl backwards, but there was a foot on his back.

"Good riddansh, freak." He heard from behind him, before being thrust forward. The water came up to hit him like a cold slap in the face as he fell.

CHAPTER 04

"Is he dead?"

"I'm not sure... Touch him."

"*You* touch him!"

"Should we tell Brian?"

Damon's mind swam. *Am I dead?* He coughed and opened his eyes. He was lying on his back, and the sky above him was bright and blue again. He squinted at the sun and covered his eyes with the back of his palm. His skin felt clammy and cold, and his arm felt almost heavy to move, like it was soaked with water. He could taste the salt in the air. He sucked in, trying to get a good breath, but he could still feel water in his lungs. He turned his head to the side, feeling like he was about to throw up. It was then that he became aware of the big furry orange face looking down on him.

Damon tried to scream, but only a hacking watery cough came out. He sputtered and rolled onto his arms and knees, heaving salt water from his lungs. He looked up, expecting the hallucination creature to be gone, but instead, it *waved* at him with a big orange paw.

And that was the *second* time Damon ever ran away. Scrambling, he crawled as fast as fast as he could back towards the waterfront, which turned out, was not very fast. The world spun and he toppled to one side. Lying there groaning, he kicked with one foot at the sand. That was when he remembered the storm, and the fight, and... the *ghost*? *What had the Admiral called it? The Dutchman?* His head hurt just thinking about it.

"I don't think he wants to be here, Lionel."

"Tough luck for him then."

Damon felt two hairy arms pick him up from the sand. He squirmed, but couldn't break free of the creature's grasp. Damon was carried like a baby for what seemed like an hour, but was likely only a few minutes. He felt himself being placed back on the ground, with his back against a large oak tree. Damon coughed again. His head was clear enough now to take a good luck at the other man, and he gasped when he did.

The man, or perhaps, the *creature* standing before him looked like a mixture between a cat and a cow. He had two arm, two legs, and stood upright like a person; but instead of pink skin, he was covered in a thick layer of dark orange fur. His arms ended in muscular cat paws, and his face had a slight snout to it. He wore a tattered white t-shirt and baggy tan shorts, with a hole in the back for a short furry tail to protrude from. His whiskers swayed in the breeze, hanging above a mouth twisted up in a concerned expression.

"Are you good?"

Damon was confused. The cat-man's mouth didn't move at all. *Is this telepathy?* He thought. But then Damon realized: there was *two* voices. It wasn't the cat-man speaking. Damon looked around, but he couldn't figure out where the other voice was coming from.

"Down here, dammit!"

Damon looked down beside him. Amongst the leaves stood a miniature man. A very *annoyed* miniature man.

"About time you woke up."

Damon scooped the tiny man up and held him in his palm, forgetting all about the other absurdity he had been greeted with. He stared in wonder at the man, as if he were a figurine. "You're so... small."

That seemed to offend the little man. He gestured to himself with his thumb. "I'll have you know that I'm the biggest Thumb there's been in over 100 hundred years. I'm four and a half inches."

Damon couldn't help but let out a snicker. "That's still small in my book."

The small man frowned, taking it as a slight. From his belt he pulled a sewing needle, and jammed the pointed end hard into the meat of Damon's palm.

"Theo!" Called out the cat-man, disapprovingly.

Yowling, Damon instinctively jerked his hand away. Theo fell, but bounced softly in the leaves below. The cat-man looked exasperated, bending down, he scooped him up in a hairy orange claw, where the small man was brushing dirt of his jacket while muttering curses under his breath.

"Put me down, Beast," he said.

He frowned. "You know I hate being called that."

Theo shrugged. "You're a Beast, I'm a Thumb", same way it's been for generations. You're going to have to come to terms with it eventually Lionel." He looked at Damon as Lionel placed him gently back on the grass. "And you're a..." he paused, waving his hand in a way that said he wanted Damon to finish.

"...Grimm?" he said, more a question than an answer.

Both men stared at him for a long while before speaking again.

"What did you say?" Lionel pressed him.

Shit! thought Damon, remembering his cover. "Black," he said. "I'm Dexter Black."

The others looked at each other, then back at him.

"No", Theo shook his head. "You said Grimm. Your name is Grimm..." He turned back towards Lionel. "Do you think he hit his head?"

Maybe I did, thought Damon. "Are you guys Navy?"

That made them laugh. "Do we *look* Navy to you?" Lionel laughed again. *I don't know*, thought Damon. *Admiral Carley looks pretty gnarly.*

"I don't think I quite meet the height requirement," Theo mused.

Damon coughed and rose shakily to his feet. "Then I'm Damon Grimm."

"I think we should take him to Nelda." Lionel said to Theo, as the two contemplated. Theo nodded. "You'd better come with us," said Lionel, placing Theodore on his shoulder.

As Lionel led him up from the coastline, Damon found himself in a wood similar to that of the Black Forest back home, but this one was much thinner. Within fifteen minutes, he could see the other side. Shielding his eyes from the light, he walked into a clearing, and was stunned by what he saw.

Did I drown... is this real? His head still swam.

The clearing was roughly fifty or sixty acres in size. Most of it was just grass and farms, but a small village sat nestled around a small creek. Even more magnificent, atop the sole hill stood a great stone castle. Lionel caught him staring.

"That's Grimmhaven."

Damon furrowed his brow. "What did you say?"

"Grimmhaven." He smiled. "You heard me. But we aren't going there yet, we need to get you checked out."

Instead of the castle, Lionel led Damon into the village. All the while he was marvelling at everything around him. The village, the castle, the cattish man he was following, and the bite sized one riding on his shoulder. Crossing the river, he noticed a crudely made sign with the word "Babblebrook" carved in large letters; though it was so old, the letters were almost too scuffed to read. The sign was apt though; the brook did babble. The bridge itself was made of thick dark pine logs, obviously taken from the surrounding forest of similar trees.

Lionel was leading him to a house with a poppy garden, but Theo said something to him and they stopped in front of a house a few houses shy. The house, more of a cabin in reality, had its front door swung wide open, and a window smashed out.

"Shit," said Lionel under his breath as he walked inside. Damon, not really knowing what else to do, followed suite.

Inside was cozy enough. Stone hearth, a few chairs, and a large dog sleeping in the middle of the room. Damon even thought to pet it, until it rolled over to reveal to great goat horn and a shaggy humanlike face. He leapt back, and nearly tripped on an empty bottle. Lionel went to the hearth, bent down, and picked a syringe from the ashes.

"Detomidine", he said with disgust as he threw it into a corner.

"What's that"

Lionel dusted himself off from the soot. "Horse tranquilizer."

As Damon tried to process that, Lionel was attempting to wake the monster from his drugged stupor.

"Gruff, you lout, get up!"

Not in that state he won't.

The big lump on the floor began to stir, and cough. A flea leapt out of his fur.

Theo jumped back. To him, the flea must have been the size of a small dog. "Good grief."

Damon's head hurt. He wasn't sure if it was from this or the wreck, or the fight, or all three. "Who's this guy."

"His name is Gruff." Lionel gave him a slight kick. Not enough to hurt him, just to get him up.

Gruff snorted and stirred again.

Damon looked to the syringe again. "All out of weed?"

"Stuff won't work on him." Lionel turned towards the door. "I told Nelda to stop bringing him that stuff."

"What about Gruff?" Theo asked as Lionel placed him back on his shoulder.

"Leave him. It's not the first time he's been like this and it won't be the last."

Damon took one last look at the beastly thing before leaving. He didn't like the look of him. Reminded him too much of his childhood.

As they walked up to the house with the poppy garden, Damon wondered what he'd be greeted by next. *A witch? Maybe a man with wings? Two-heads?* It turned out to be none of the above. The girl who opened the door was a sweet young thing in a white frock with short auburn hair and freckles. More importantly, the first *normal* person he'd seen in a while.

She looked puzzled to Damon. "It's not often we have guests."

Damon raised an eyebrow. "When's the last time?"

She shrugged. "Never."

"Nelda, this is Damon. Damon; Nelda. We need you to take a look at him."

She bit her lip. "He looks fine to me."

Lionel pushed past her into the cabin. "We're hoping that's the case."

Damon, unsure what to do, followed. Nelda let him, but gave him a disapproving look as he went. "It's not like you to barge into homes with strangers in tow, Lionel. What's got your goose?"

"There are no *strangers* on the island. Except him." He pulled a lab coat from a coatrack and held it out for Nelda. "We found him on the beach, I want to make sure he isn't sick… in the body *or* in the head."

Nelda cocked her head at him. "You do remember that even with that on I'm not a doctor?"

"I do, but you're the closest thing we have. Didn't your father train you? That's what you always like telling us."

She rolled her eyes and took the coat

"Just how old are you guys, anyway?" Damon asked, it only really donning on him now that these may not even be adults.

"Sixteen," answered Nelda.

"Twenty," said Lionel, give or take.

"Same," Theo answered.

"Are your parents around somewhere"

Theo and Lionel looked at each other. Neither answered.

"Take off your shirt." Nelda stood over him, a stethoscope in hand.

"Do you even know what that's for?" Damon gave a hacking cough.

"I was about to check your lungs, but I think you just answered my question."

Damon coughed again, reeling over himself so much that his pendant came out from beneath his uniform. It dangled in front as he caught his breath.

"What's that?" Asked Lionel.

"Its mine is what it is." He slipped it back under his shirt., but Lionel wasn't about to let it stay at that. He walked over to Damon and held out a hand. "Let me see that."

"No," but he sighed and took it out anyway, slipping the cord from around his neck and placing it in Lionel's paw.

The setting sun was shining in through the window, and Lionel held up the pendent between his thumb and forefinger, squinting at it in the light. Then, to Damon's absolute horror, he crushed the acrylic in his paw, picking out the strands of hair from within. Even Nelda seemed shocked.

"What did you do that for?"

Damon was ready to deck Lionel across his snout, cat claws or no cat claws, but another bout of coughing stopped him.

"Where did you get this?" Asked Lionel, seemingly stunned.

Damon wiped his mouth. "Those are hairs from my dead mother, you bastard, now give them back." He could feel tears welling in his eyes.

"No." said Lionel.

"No, you won't give them back?" *Does this guy want me to kill him?*

"No, these aren't hairs; they're *fur*. Lionel held the small clump up to his arm. "My fur."

CHAPTER 05

"What do you mean it's *your* fur?" Damon stared baffled at Lionel. "Unless you're my mother; which I seriously doubt." He pushed past Nelda and attempted a swing at Lionel, but Damon was slow and sluggish, and Lionel's reflexes were good.

"Do you ever stop trying to punch people?" quipped Theodore.

Lionel shushed him and looked Damon in the eye. "I know how it must seem... but it would make sense if you're a Grimm."

"Grimm?" Nelda looked puzzled, but realization came over her face when she looked at Damon. "You don't think-"

"He might be." Lionel cut her off.

"Might be *what*?" Damon was getting sick and tired of them not telling him things.

"I think it's best we show you, rather than tell you."

As they the four of them left the cabin, they watched as a younger group of lads attempted to wrestle a very agitated Gruff from his own cabin.

Nelda crossed her arms. "Looks like the high wore off."

Gruff roared and knocked one of the boys clean off his feet and into the brook. Another got a lick of Gruff's horn across the cheek.

Damon winced. "Shouldn't we help them?"

Lionel shook his head no. "Those boys are our guard force here on the island. It's not the first time they've had to deal with Gruff, and they *do not* like anyone showing them up.

Lionel turned away and motioned for Damon to follow. Damon stood in place. Looking nervously over toward where the three boys feebly attempted to wrangle the goat-man to the ground. It reminded Damon of a bully, throwing the younger children around because they could. He could feel his blood starting to boil as he watched.

"Damon!" It was Nelda this time. "They'll be fine."

Damon coughed, and continued to stand in place. Nelda sighed and walked back over to him, placing a hand on his shoulder. "They're fine, lets -" a sickening *CRACK* cut her off.

Damon watched in horror as Gruff used his bare hands to tear one of the boy's arms clean off at the elbow. Damon shoved Nelda aside and charged headlong at the beast below.

The two other boys were still attempting to wrangle Gruff. Damon noticed one was now pointing a pistol, but for some reason hesitating to fire it. The other only seemed to carry a dagger. Damon had nothing. His chest hurt as he ran, but that didn't stop him. Leaping from a stone ridge just above the others, Damon landed atop Gruff's back, wrapping his arms around his hairy neck. Gruff was big, but his balance was terrible. The two spun twice round as Gruff tried to grab at the man attached to his back. Damon wasn't letting go. Gruff staggered to one side, and lost his balance. The two sprawled headlong into the brook. Damon felt the familiar sting of being doused in cold water for the second time that day.

The brook was deep enough that Damon didn't scrape against the bottom, although he knew that he was close. He had let go of the goat and was now being carried downstream. His ears were plugged with water, and his eyes closed, so he had no idea where Gruff was. A paw gripped him by his collar and dragged him up onto the bank. Damon kicked out instinctively, but stopped, when he opened his eyes to see Lionel standing above him.

"What the hell, man?"

"What do you mean?" Lionel looked confused. "Did you *not* want out of the water?"

Damon spit out water and rose to his knees. "That thing just killed a man! And you keep it around?"

Lionel furrowed his brow. "Gruff's never killed anyone."

Damon snapped. "You don't survive getting your arm ripped off.

"I do." The voice came from behind him.

Damon turned to see a boy smiling at him. His right arm was severed at the bicep, and he carried the arm with him in his left. Damon looked to the stump. There was no blood, no muscle, not even a bone. *Only... splinters?* The boy caught him staring.

"Nothing a little wood glue can't fix." He smiled and held out the severed arm for Damon to shake, grinning as he did it. "I'm Woody."

Damon raised an eyebrow. "I can see that." He looked around. "Where are your friends?" *And Gruff for that matter.*

Woody chuckled. "Probably off pouting about you showing them up."

As Woody went off to find his friends, Damon joined Lionel and Nelda to wherever they were meaning to take him. Eventually, Damon found himself being led up a small flight of wooden stairs just inside the treeline. At the top was a small white church. Beside it lay a graveyard, surrounded by a rusted iron fence. Lionel took Damon to the gravesite, and grunted as he wrangled the rusted gate open.

"Been a while since anyone been in here?" Damon asked.

"It's only been a while for the living." Lionel answered, surprisingly ominously.

Damon counted at least two or three hundred headstones. As he walked down the lines, he had an eerie feeling like he belonged here somehow. He did not like that feeling. Damon turned to leave, but Lionel stopped him and pointed to two gravestones that loomed larger and more central than the others. Sheepishly, he approached them. He was surprised to find that the one on the left read "Jakob Grimm" and the one on the right read "Wilhelm Grimm." He puzzled for a moment before turning towards Lionel. Damon was about to say something but stopped, finally understanding.

"Its *you*," he said. "You're..."

"Fairy tales?" Lionel finished. You could say that.

Am I? No, thought Damon. *I can't be, I'm just a normal person. I'm just Damon. Damon-*

"Grimm," Damon said. "You said I was a Grimm."

Lionel scratched at his chin. "Well, I said that you *might* be a Grimm."

"Only one way to know for sure." It was Nelda. She was leading someone from the church. It was an elderly man, carrying a tome larger than his head in his crinkled paper hands. Bald spots peppered his brow amongst wisps of thin white hairs. One of the lenses of his spectacles was chipped at the corner, and on a dropped shoulder sat Theo Thumb.

Damon looked to Lionel. "First old person I've seen all day."

That made Lionel chuckle. "Actually, he's younger that anyone else here."

Damon's face twisted in confusion. "When was he born?"

"Monday," Lionel answered simply.

Nelda pointed, and the big old man lay the book on a nearby stump. Nelda thanked him and flipped to a page about a third of the way through. The paper was yellow and cracked.

"Come read this, Damon."

"What is it?"

"Read," the skeletal man boomed in a gravely voice.

Damon knelt in front of the book. The headers were in German, so he could not read them, but he understood one word: Grimm.

"It's a family tree," he said, with sudden realization.

Damon traced his finger down the lines, until he found the name "Jacob John Grimm", there was no picture, but Damon had a feeling. He looked up.

"That's my grandfathers name."

Nelda chewed her lip. "I hoped it might." She was obviously pondering something.

Lionel must have been thinking the same thing. "How is it that you'd wash up here?" He was scratching his chin again. "That's an incredible coincidence."

"I'm not sure, all I remember was this... thing attacking our ship. For some reason it wanted me."

"What kind of thing?" Asked Lionel.

"A ghost. I think the Admiral called it The Dutchman."

Lionel and Nelda looked at each other.

Damon frowned. "You don't mean - that's the *actual* Dutchman? The old sailor's tale?"

Lionel scratched at his chin. "Well, someone descended from the original."

Damon looked at him confused. "How does a ghost have kids?"

Lionel crossed his arms and raised an eyebrow. "Is that really the most pressing question you have right now?"

Damon looked around. "Does that make all of you the descendants of fairy tales.

Nelda nodded. "Fairy tales, folklore, myths, legends..."

"But... how has no one found you?"

It was Theo who answered. "You already met our defense mechanism." He smiled. "You'd be surprised at how many superstitious sailors stay away from cursed waters."

"And the few who do come into contact with our green friend out there."

It was while he pondered that he noticed a gravestone nearby labelled "King Beast" The face carved into the stone was a mixture of a cat and a cow, with two horns on his forehead and a crown resting on his brow. As grotesque as the caricature looked, the face still seemed calm, and authoritative. Damon looked to Lionel and pointed at the stone.

"This was your father?"

"Six-times Great-Grandfather, actually", he corrected, smiling warmly at the grave.

The one beside it depicted a beautiful woman, old, but handsome, with hair down part her shoulders and a rose in her hand. Inscribed below were the words "Queen Beauty"

"You're descended from the Beast."

"Up until now did you just think I was very hairy, or that Theo Thumb was just very short?"

"Or that I was just very pretty and smart?" Nelda added.

Damon looked over his shoulder at her. "Who are you supposed to be from, you just look like a normal girl to me."

"I'm Nelda Knowall." She did a little curtsy. When Damon didn't look any less confused, she rolled her eyes. "No one has ever heard of my story."

That gave Damon pause. "Just how many of you are here?"

Lionel smiled. "Let me show you."

CHAPTER 06

"Welcome to Grimmhaven!" Lionel motioned with his arm to the great door of the Castle on the hill.

Lionel and Damon had begun their trek towards the looming structure while the sky was still light, but now dusk was setting in as they came upon the grand oak door. Theo had gotten to ride on Lionel's shoulder, and Damon was beginning to envy the little man as his calves and feet were having a contest on which could hurt more. Nelda had parted with them a while back, and was fetching everyone else on the island to come and meet the new arrival. The thought both excited and terrified Damon. He'd never been one for being the center of attention, but at the same time, he was excited to see what other colourful inhabitants the island had to offer.

"Grimmhaven?" Damon repeated the name silently to himself. He ran a hand against the stone and wondered just how long the castle had stood here. As he pondered, his stomach growled and he realized that he hadn't eaten since before being thrown from the Blacktooth; and that was almost twenty-four hours ago by now. Damon turned sheepishly to Lionel, almost ashamed to ask in light of everything else.

"Is there a chance of getting something to eat in there?"

Lionel nodded. "Of course." He opened the door and ushered Damon inside.

The castle was grand to Damon, but still small as far as castles were concerned. Most of the main floor was taken up by a single dining chamber. An archway to the kitchen was near the back, and in each corner was a door leading up into one of the castle's four towers. When Damon looked up, he could see what might have been a library peaking out from a second floor.

As Damon looked around, he began to marvel. The main dining chamber was huge, like nothing he had ever seen before. Eight massive pillars carved from raw stone ran two-by-two from the grand front door to the ornate hearth burning near the kitchen at the back. A huge wooden longtable was set between the pillars, running from nearly one end of the room to the other. Rows of tall stained-glass windows lined each wall like ribs. Each depicted a scene in time. As Lionel led him into the room, Damon noticed the pane nearest him; An old man with a head like a lion's was thrusting a golden sword into the chest of a serpent. Damon couldn't help but notice the resemblance that Lionel had to the man.

The chamber itself was void of any people, other than the three of them, but Damon counted near half a hundred chairs at the table. And judging by the spacing between the seats, it looked to Damon as if there was room for half a hundred more. As Lionel walked up to the longtable, Theodore hopped from his shoulder and landed on it like a mouse. Lionel moved up beside him again. "I hope you're ready."

"To eat?" Damon asked hopefully.

Lionel smiled. "To meet everyone."

The grand doors to the mess chamber opened once again, and all at once, the room started to fill with a cast of characters. Some looked like the everyday people you'd see on the street; but others were anything but. Damon was surprised to find he even knew who a few of them were, or at least, who their *ancestors* were.

The first ones inside were a group of three boys, laughing to one another has they came into the chamber. Damon recognized them from before. Woody had a bandage wrapped tightly around his right forearm and a sling holding it to his chest. One of the other boys, the chubby one with a pistol on his belt, had gauze taped across one cheek. The third was wearing an interesting green outfit complete with a pointed green hood. Damon thought he looked right out of the middle ages.

It was the chubby boy who first noticed Damon. He was laughing at something Woody had said when their eyes locked and he stopped. The other boys followed his gaze to where Damon stood, and all three hushed. Damon didn't like the look in the chubby boy's eye, and prepared himself for trouble. The boy must have seen something in Damon too, and his hand went to his holster. *Great. Just great.* Damon thought as the three moved towards him. Woody gave a friendly wave with his good hand as they got closer, but the Chubby one glared at him and he stopped. Lionel cleared his throat before anyone else had the chance to say or do something they would regret.

"Damon, I'd like you to meet Sean of Nottingham, or Notty as we like to call him." He then motioned to the boy dressed in the green hood. "And this Piedmont Piper; or Monty, if you would. And I believe you've already met Woody?"

Damon gave them a look over. "Charmed."

Notty frowned and pushed past Lionel, getting uncomfortably close to Damon. "Don't think we didn't see what you did down by the river with the goat."

Damon raised an eyebrow. He could feel blood rising to his cheeks. "You mean *help* you?" Damon remembered Lionel talking about how much they hated that, and it showed on Notty's face.

Notty grit his teeth. "We never asked for it, and we didn't need it. He took his hand from his holster and poked a finger into Damon's chest. "This island runs because we keep the order. If people see you showing us up, they may lose confidence in that ability. Understand?"

Oh, I'll show you understanding. I understand that I should have just let you fuckers get gored. Damon made a step forward, but Lionel stepped on his toes with a clawed foot, and he sat down into a seat, holding in a yelp.

"He understands," said Lionel with a smile.

With every new face that came up to greet him, Damon was having a harder and harder time remembering everyone's names. By the time Lionel was shutting the front door to Grimmhaven Castle, Damon had been introduced to around twenty people, but he could only remember about five. It was easier with the stranger looking of the bunch. One of the residents he had met was a girl named Charlotte. At first glance she looked liked the typical teenage emo girl, with long black hair covering her eyes, and pasty white skin. But from her back protruded four massive spider legs came through holes cut into the back of her black jacket. Even stranger was a resident named Elliot, who had nut brown skin and two deer antlers protruding from his head. Damon had also noticed that his eyes shone a brilliant silver.

The smell of roasting meat and garlic butter wafted in from the kitchens and reminded Damon of how hungry he was. He changed seats to one near the far end of the table, as to not draw too much attention to himself. But that was impossible, the residents here hadn't seen anyone new in all their time on the island, and none were about to let go of the chance to talk to someone up from the outside. Many tried to take the seat next to Damon, but one was lucky enough to slip through the rest and get there first.

"What's your uniform for?" A bubbly boy around ten years old named Zack sat down next to Damon and started ruffling at his sleeve.

"Um." Damon stuttered, not entirely sure how to react. "It's Navy."

"Oooooh!" said the young boy excitedly. "Are you a Captain? Do you kill pirates? Do you -"

"That's enough, Zack." One of the other boys pulled the kid from Damon's arm and scooted him over to the next chair. "Sorry about him, most of his knowledge comes from children's books."

This boy was older, maybe fifteen or sixteen with short black hair and a pair of round glasses that were chipped at the bottom of one lens.

"Thanks," said Damon, then paused before saying. "Sorry, I forgot your name."

The boy chuckled. 'I get it, it's a lot to take in for one day." He reached out a hand. "I'm Marlin."

Damon shook it. "Marlin like the magician?"

"That was *Merlin*, but yes, he was some old ancestor of mine."

That piqued Damon's interest. "So, you can do magic tricks?"

Marlin smiled and pointed to where Theo was sitting on the long table chatting with Nelda. With a snap of his fingers, the small man began to levitate into the air. Theo began flailing his limbs and cursing at Marlin, to the merriment of the rest of the audience.

"I'm going to beat your ass wizard!" Theo yelled as he rolled in the air.

"You can't even reach my ass!" Marlin quipped as the others laughed again.

When the dinner was finally served, Damon was surprised to see that there was much less food than he'd expected. There was chicken, and fresh bread, and some vegetables, but only about half his plate ended up getting filled, with no chance of seconds. Damon wolfed it down in minutes and was still very much hungry when he finished, but thought it best to not make a stink. Damon licked grease from his fingers and looked around the room. They had accidentally given Zack an extra leg of chicken and Damon stared at it with envy. *Lucky little bastard*, he thought.

One thing Damon had been wondering about since the start of the dinner was the almost throne-like chair that headed the longtable, looking down it rather than across. At first, he assumed that the chair was empty because it would be rude for anyone to sit in it; a sort of "no one is better than the rest" type thing. But as the dinner had gone on, he had become aware that the chair to its immediate left was also empty, and Notty, who sat to the throne's right, had been very quiet the whole dinner. Damon cleared his throat and turned to Lionel, who was gnawing on a chicken bone.

"Who sits up there?" he asked.

Lionel didn't even have to look up to know which seat Damon spoke of.

"Brian." It seemed like Lionel didn't really want to talk about it.

Not a very regal sounding name. "Brian who?" Damon pushed

"Brian Rose," Lionel answered after a pause. "He's our de-facto leader, if you want to call him that. He runs things, or more accurately he just kind of makes sure we all keep out of each other's hair."

"Seems like a leader should come see the new arrival to his island, hey?"

"Nelda asked, but he said he needed to consider some things before coming."

"And the other empty chair? Did Brian not let his girl come meet me without him there?"

"That seat is for his sister actually."

Damon gave Lionel a look.

"Not like *that*, perv." He through the bone into a bucket near the middle of the table. "Briar is his twin sister. They're just close is all. They confide in each other, you know?"

As if on cue, the great doors opened again and Damon turned to see a man and woman enter. "That them?" Damon asked.

"That's them." Lionel raised a hand in a wave. "Brian!"

The man walked past him without so much as a look. He certainly *looked* the role of leader. He wore gilded bronze chest plate armour decorated with metal roses, and at his hip was a scabbard of red leather. His hair was a reddish brown and it came down to just over the ears of his pink freckled face. All together, it made him look half the boy and half the warrior. The room went hush as he walked up to Damon.

"Umm. Hi?" Damon looked to Lionel for reassurance but got none. "I'm Damon Grimm."

"I've heard," said Brian.

Damon searched for something to say. "Nice Castle you've got here."

"It's not mine. It's all of ours."

Oh boy, this guy's going to be hard to talk to. "Did you want something to eat?" Damon already knew he didn't like Brian, but didn't want to burn bridges just yet.

Brian nodded, and walked to the end of the longtable to take his seat at the helm. The woman, who could have only been his twin sister, followed a few steps behind. She looked just like Brian, other than the breasts and the long curls in her hair. Instead of armour, she wore a flowing red silk dress, and a crown of roses atop her head. As she passed Damon, she gave him a coy smile and a slight nod, twirling a strand of her hair. Damon felt his face flush. Lionel must have seen it too. He leaned over to Damon and whispered

"Don't even try it, Brian *will* kill you."

He can try, Damon thought. *He can certainly* try.

✳ ✳ ✳

Although most of the group had already finished eating by the time Brian and Briar had began. Woody had taken his leave at Brian's behest to go bring food down into the Castle's dungeon for Gruff, who was noticeably absent at the table.

When Damon had heard that, he'd immediately become concerned. "Dungeon?"

Lionel shrugged. "Dungeon, holding cell, apartment suite, doesn't really matter what you call it; it's just somewhere with metal doors that can contain Gruff while he blows off steam."

"So, he's the only one down there?"

"At the moment yes, but ever now and again someone will get into a fight and Notty or Monty will chuck them down there for a time out. You ever try living in an enclosed space with the same thirty-odd people for years? We don't always get along."

"Years? No. Damon admitted. "But I do know what it's like to live on a boat for a few months with the same crew." He could see that Lionel about to ask him about that, but it wasn't something he wanted to talk about so he quickly changed the subject. "Anyone else not here that I should know about?

Lionel scratched at his chin. "Well, I suppose Dora."   He shrugged. "But I doubt you'll meet her."

"Why's that?"

Lionel took a sip of water from his glass. "Ever heard of Pandora's Box?"

"No"

"Every disease known to man tucked inside it, you open the box, and... well... you don't *want* to open the box. That's the point of the story. You get near Dora, touch her, breath in the air she breathes, you get sick. Very sick. We keep her quarantined at the far end of the island. If she needs to talk to one of us, she has a hazmat suit she can wear, but she rarely comes by, she's grown accustomed to living on her own."

Damon frowned. "That's so sad." But he still had to ask. "Has anyone ever gotten sick?"

Lionel grinned. "Monty once kissed her on a dare, he turned green and shit water for three days. Lucky for him that was back when Nelda's dad was on the island. He fixed Monty up, made sure he didn't wind up dead. Notty ended up in the dungeon for a few days for daring him, but I think Dora felt more guilty than he did."

Something Lionel had said made Damon begin to wonder again. "Nelda's father? Where did he go. I still haven't seen anyone older than me on this island, and I'm only twenty-two."

Lionel took another long sip. Damon was starting to suspect it wasn't actually *water* in the glass. "I think its best Brian was the one to tell you about that. Lionel got up. "It's late, I think I'm going to head in for the night. If you need me, my place is the one three doors to the right of Nelda's. He paused. "Try not to need me until after the sun comes up, OK?"

Damon waved goodbye to him. In truth, he was nervous to see him go. Without him, Damon felt lost with the group of strangers around him. He scanned the table for Nelda or Theodore, but neither were still there. In fact, half the residents had gone home. Damon looked out the stained-glass windows to see the pitch black of midnight. The only light came from the candles burning inside Grimmhaven. Damon stretched and thought about sleep. He was tired too, but it hadn't occurred to him until now that he didn't have a place to stay.

He got up to ask Brian about it, but the de-facto leader was deep in conversation with Notty. Briar looked as though she would have shown him to his room, but Lionel's warning seemed to have stuck in his head. He looked around to anyone else who could help him.

"Marlin?" The boy turned to look at Damon. "Do you think you could find me somewhere I could sleep?"

Marlin adjusted his glasses. "That would be up to Brian."

Damn, thought Damon. He cleared his throat and went over to them.

"Um, Brian?" The armoured boy looked at him, annoyed.

"What is it?"

"I was thinking of hitting the hay. Any chance of a bed?"

Brian tapped his fingers on the table. "You'll stay in the dungeons tonight.

The dunge- what!? Damon thought he must have misheard.

"Its nothing personal," Brian tried to reassure him. "But we don't know you. I'd feel better if I knew my people could sleep easy."

As angry as Damon was, he really did understand where Brian was coming from. He let Notty lead him down the tower stairs to underneath the mess chamber. As they went, Damon could hear the sound of snoring coming up like a foghorn. But other than that, Lionel wasn't kidding when he shrugged the dungeon off as an apartment suite. It was warm, and the cell had a bed at least, if not a window. Damon could make it work. At least for a night.

"You comfortable?" Notty asked, surprising Damon with how genuine he sounded.

Damon stopped himself from making a snide comment. "No, I should be good." Notty nodded and shut the cell door. "How's the cheek?" Damon asked.

Notty scoffed. "Not as bad as the last time Gruff got me." He raised his shirt slightly to show off an ugly red scar the size of a quarter just above the waistline from where something had pieced the skin.

Damon grimaced. "Is it work it keeping him around?" He tried to lighten the comment with a joke. "Can't you guys vote him off the island?" It went over the boy's head, understandably, since there was no TV on the island.

"We're all family here. Gruff's a troublemaker, but we look out for one another."

Damon nodded his understanding. He heard the lock click shut and watched as Notty disappeared from view.

CHAPTER 07

"Damon awoke in a groggy confusion of not knowing where he was. But as his eyes adjusted and his mind began to gain consciousness, he remembered the situation he'd found himself in. The dungeons remained dark, but without windows that could mean midnight or midday. Slowly, Damon rose to his feet and walked to the barred metal door. He tried the handle, but it was locked. *Damn*, he thought. *I really have to pee.*

"Up, are you?" The voice came from around the corner. A boy got up from a stool and walked over dangling keys.

"Woody?" Damon asked.

Woody looked hurt. "Ya, who'd you think I was?"

Damon looked down to where Woody had two unbandaged arms. "You're not wearing your sling."

Woody unlocked the door. "Fast-setting wood glue; twenty-four hour. I'm right as rain." He smiled.

Damon grabbed a candle from where it sat, still sleepy, he brought it around without looking and nearly hit Woody in the face. The boy caught him by the wrist and looked Damon in the eye. "Careful with that."

Damon nodded and lowered the flame. After Woody showed Damon where he could relieve himself, he took him back into Babblebrook to find Lionel. Damon judged it to be around noon by the look of the sun. It was still sunny, but clouds were beginning to role in and he could feel a chill down his back. He'd have to remember to ask Lionel for some extra clothes when he got down there.

Damon knocked on the door. Lionel answered right away, his one arm caught in the sleeve of a blue sweatshirt, his claw snagged in the fabric.

Lionel glanced over at Woody. "Game starts in ten, you playing today?"

Woody shrugged. "Maybe."

"Game?" asked Damon

"Oh, I suppose you wouldn't know." His claw finally unsnagged itself. "Every week we all have a big capture the flag game out in the woods. It's a little juvenile in truth, but it's tradition and it passes the time. Care to join?"

No. Damon thought. "Yes," he said.

***

"Alright." Brian was addressing the crowd. "I'll go over the rules for those of us playing for the first time." He looked directly at Damon. "And those of us who seem to have trouble… *remembering* them." He looked not-so-subtly at Notty and Monty. They were out in the middle of the forest, on the opposite side of the town which Damon had arrived from. Everyone who was at dinner seemed to be here. Damon scratched at his chest. He was wearing a blue woollen shirt that was too big for him. It was the only other thing Lionel had that was blue.

Each resident was wearing some article of clothing that's colour showed their team. There was red, blue, purple, yellow, and green. Lionel had taken Damon as part of his team, the Blue team, along with Theodore, Charlotte the spider girl, and a girl named Nikki. Damon noticed that Brian was wearing red, for the "rose" he assumed. Briar, unsurprisingly, was next time him in a red frock. Her long red curls had been tied back into a long braid and pinned to her head with a clip adorned with a rose. She gave Damon a little smile when she caught him looking at her.

"No," whispered Lionel, not even looking at Damon.

"I didn't even say anything." Damon protested. *I was only thinking it.*

Brian placed a hand on his hip. He wasn't wearing his sword today, thank goodness. "Did you hear what I said Damon?"

"Hmm?" Damon looked over at him, blissfully unaware. Briar gave a slight giggle and Brian sighed.

"Again, the goal is to capture all the other team's flags. You can hide the flag anywhere aboveground within the forest. You're all wearing ribbons of your colour. If someone grabs that ribbon off of you, you're out of the game. No hiding your ribbons." He turned again to Notty before adding: "and for the love of God, no breaking someone's nose to get their ribbon."

"Any questions, Damon?" It was Briar who asked. It was the first time he'd heard her speak. Her voice was soft and sweet and warm.

Damon smirked. "Ya, what do we get if we win?"

Brian laughed. For you? "I'll let you sleep in the tower tonight." He paused. "But if we win, you have to sleep in the same cell as Gruff."

That seemed to make everyone laugh. "Deal," said Damon.

Nelda rolled her eyes and groaned. "And if any of the *other* teams win? I suppose we just get bragging rights?" She was wearing a purple tank top, the same colour as the man who Damon had met in the graveyard.

Brian looked to her. "Exactly, Nelly."

Nelda hopped up from the stump she was sitting on, and plucked a wooden stick with a purple bandana tied to the end from where it was driven into the ground. "Call me Nelly again, and I'll let Gruff into *your* room." With that she turned and marched off into the forest, with the other residents in purple following behind.

"I guess the game is on," said Lionel as he picked the blue flag from the dirt.

"Where to?" asked Damon.

"Damon, the point is to *hide* the flag, not tell them where we're going with it."

Right, he thought as he followed Lionel out into the brush. He waited until they were all well out of earshot before he asked again. "So, what's the game plan?"

The girl named Nikki chuckled. "Easy, the yellow team never wins once Zack is out of the game, the green team always hides their flag somewhere by the waterfall, and Nelda's team is never good at finding anything. Just worry about Brian's band and you'll be fine."

Damon gave her a smile. "I don't think I met you last night." He stuck out a hand. "I'm Damon."

"I know." Nikki took his hand, her skin was cold, almost icy to the touch. "I'm Nikki Frost."

The five of them came upon an old half-dead oak tree just south of the brook, ravaged by the elements. The lower branches had all died and cracked off, but the canopy was still green, although not seemingly long for this world.

"Charlotte?" Lionel handed her the flagpole.

Damon was taken aback as he watched the shy girl leap ten feet into the air, and grab the trunk of the tree with her arachnid legs. Then she bounded up again, catching one of the higher branches, and crawled her way into the top leaves, disappearing from view.

The sight of her both fascinated and horrified Damon. After a few moments, the tree rustled and Charlotte came leaping thirty feet to the ground, and then brushed the hair from her eyes.

"So now what? Should one of us stay here and guard?"

Lionel shook his head "And give away the position? No. Theodore and I will head down to the waterfall. You and Nikki head towards the meadow, Nelda's usually somewhere over there. Charlotte can start scoping the trees." He turned to leave but stopped. 'Oh, and Damon?"

"Ya?"

"Remember, it's your neck on the line of we don't win. I'm sure Gruff would love a roommate." He grinned and walked off.

"Come on!" said Nikki, grabbing his arm and running off with Damon in tow.

* * *

It was a good twenty minutes before they even saw another person. Three, in fact. From where they sat up on the ridge, they could see Marlin and Zack searching amongst the trees, and Woody not-so-subtly hidden, waiting to pounce on whichever one came close.

"So, should we go down there?"

Nikki held up a hand. Too shush him. "Look out!"

Damon felt something, or *someone*, barrel into him. The two went tumbling over the side of the ridge into the brush below. Woody shot up from his hiding place, startled. Marlin and Zack stopped in their tracks. When Zack noticed Woody staring dumbfounded, he ran up behind him and snagged the red ribbon from his belt.

"Hey, no fair kid!" Woody called after him.

Damon struggled to his feet. Monty was kneeling next to him, wiping mud from his cheek. Damon instinctively wanted to punch him, but held back. Instead, he looked to his hip. The blue ribbon still hung there. But Monty lunged forward. Damon flinched backwards; but Monty hadn't moved. Confused, he looked down, to where his feet were frozen to the ground. Nikki sauntered over, smirking, and plucked the ribbon from Monty's hip.

Monty grunted. "At least get me out of this." He broke one book from the ground with the crack of the ice, but the other was stuck tight.

"Ask Woody." She laughed. "Hey, where did Marlin go?"

Damon frowned "I think that way?" He pointed down the path to the left. They followed the path until they came across a fork in the road. Damon was about to ask which way, but stopped when something caught his attention. There was a rocky outcrop to their left. At the top, hanging amongst the red leaves of a bush, swayed a red handkerchief.

Nikki grinned and gave him a tomboyish punch to the shoulder. "Nice!"

"So how do we get it down?"

Nikki brushed the light brown hair from her blue eyes. "Not sure. It's a shame Charlotte's not here."

Damon shrugged. "Well, too bad she isn't." He placed a foot onto the first rock and steadied himself with his hands. "We'll have to climb." Nikki followed after. The climb was long and tedious, but they made it to the top. Damon snagged the makeshift flag from where it lay amongst the brambles. "Do we win?" he asked. Despite himself, he was enjoying the game.

"No," Nikki said, dusting herself off. "You need all five flags to win."

"Shame," said Damon, as the two began the descent back down.

About halfway, Damon noticed a mist rolling in, and looked down at Nikki. "Does it normally fog up in these woods?"

"No?" Nikki looked up at him, confused. "Although, Marlin can make-" She was cut off as the rock beneath her slipped, and went tumbling down. Damon tried to follow after her as quick he could, but the wave of fog washed over him, and Nikki disappeared.

"Bugger!" he yelled, at no one in particular. Damon was near blinded by the fog, and the moisture in the air was making the rocks slippery. Ever so carefully, he made his way to the path below. He called out to Nikki, but heard no reply. His brain immediately went to worst-case scenario, and he frantically began prodding the ground, trying to come across his teammate.

The fog parted before him. Only slightly, but enough that Damon could see Marlin standing before him.

The boy adjusted his glasses. "It's nothing personal, Damon."

Damon stared at him wide eyed as a small spike of purple lightning arched from Marlin's fingertips into Damon's chest; knocking him on his ass as the flag went spiralling from his hand. It reminded Damon of being tazed. Then, from seemingly out of nowhere, Zack ran by him, scooping up the flag as he went, and disappearing back into the fog.

"Hey!" He called out as the boy vanished from view. He ran after in pursuit. The fog was beginning to fade, but Damon was still having trouble seeing. He listened, and when he heard footsteps to his left, he pounced. He heard an "*oof!*" as the two of them went down. But as the mist cleared, he saw that Zack did not have the flag. In fact; it wasn't even Zach beneath him.

"Looks like you caught me." Said Briar, giving him a coy smile.

Damon scrambled to his feet. "Sorry," he muttered.

Brair gave him a pouty face that ruffled her bangs. "Why?" She made a motion towards his crotch with one hand, but as she got closer, she moved it to one side and swiped the blue ribbon from off Damon's belt.

"Hey-!" he started but she cut him off.

"Sorry new boy, have fun sleeping with the goat tonight."

Damon was about to say something but was cut off again. But this time, it *was* Zack.

"ACK!" he cried as he flailed his arms wildly, stuck in what seemed to be a giant spider's web. "Lemme down!"

Charlotte stood next to him, the smallest hint of a grin on her face. She had the red flag held in one of her human hands. Lionel was walking in from up the road, triumphantly pumping three flags in his paws.

Damon smiled, but it was wiped from his face when he remembered. *Nikki!* He turned in place looking for her, and was surprised to see her beside him. She has iced one of the rocks over and was holding it to a bump on her head. She gave him a thumbs-up. "We won."

Damon looked back at Briar. This time she was pouting for real. Damon scoffed. "Tell your brother I'd like the highest room in the tower, please."

CHAPTER 08

That night, Damon found himself unable to sleep. His new quarters were nice enough; much better than what he'd had in the dungeon, and airier than what he'd had on the Blacktooth. He hadn't gotten his wish for the highest room in the castle, but near enough for him not to mind. He'd gotten the second-highest in the south-west tower. The highest was apparently owned by a boy named Astor, and the only higher room than that was in the North-East tower, which of course was occupied by Brian. Damon couldn't complain though; it was better than spending the night with Gruff, and on top of that his view of the North Sea was amazing.

The room's window had no glass and so Damon could feel the cold night air breezing on his body. Gulls squawked far off in the distance. He was initially going to draw the curtains closed to drown them out, but instead he found that he liked the look of the light of the moon cascading over the stone bricks of the floor, so he decided to leave them open. He shivered and pulled the sheets up closer to his chin. His mind was racing. Damon couldn't help but think of all the things he'd seen, all the people he'd met. A small part of him was even jealous of residents like Marlin and Nikki with their fantastical powers.

Groggy, he sat up in bed, then moved towards the table by the window where a pitcher of water and a glass rested. Damon poured himself a glass, watching the water flow from vesical to vesical and listening to its soft burble. Sighing, he raised the glass to his lips and began to drink. The sound of something landing on his windowsill startled Damon fully awake. He sputtered, and dropped the glass, shattering it against the floor. Damon looked into the shadows and saw what he first thought was a giant bird, but as his eyes adjusted, he could see that it was a man.

"Who are you?" He asked sleepily. To a normal person, the sight of a boy with wings would leave them gobsmacked. But after what Damon had seen, he was only surprised that he hadn't seen one sooner.

"Ike, the boy said, removing goggles from his eyes. "Well, Icarus, in truth. But everyone here calls me Ike."

"I'd offer you a drink, but..." Damon motioned to the shards of glass around his feet.

"Ya, sorry about that." Ike hopped down from the windowsill. The glass crunched beneath his boots as he did. "Landings are still a little hard for me."

When Ike turned his back to Damon, he could see that the boy's wings weren't attached to him, but rather made of wooden dowels and hinges, and covered in beeswax and feathers. Ike loosened some straps on his chest and the wings slumped from his back like a backpack. Ike tossed the contraption to the bed with a *FLUMP*.

"I *was* planning on sleeping on that, you know."

Ike rubbed his shoulder blade. "Not tonight you aren't, sorry Damon."

Damon rolled his eyes. "Brian that much of a sore loser?"

"Not that... Well yes, he is. But it's not that." He opened the chamber door and beckoned Damon follow him. "There's a meeting going on in the mess chamber. Come on."

Damon didn't move. "Do I have a choice?"

Ike smiled. "Nope."

When he entered the hall, he was greeting by the sight of the five or six people who he assumed to be the more "in charge" people of the island.

Brian was at his seat at the head of the table, with Notty to his right again. Briar was noticeably absent. Lionel was there, which made Damon happy, as well as Monty, and a golden-haired boy Damon couldn't seem to remember the name of. They all looked up as Damon entered the room.

"I see you've met Ike," Brian started, with little emotion.

"Ya I have," said Damon. "Although a simple knock on the door may have been easier." He paused. "Who is this guy anyway?" He asked, sticking a thumb in Ike's direction. "I thought I'd met everyone on the island."

Brian smirked and Damon noticed he was once again wearing his sword at his belt "Did you really think we'd let you wander the island alone and unsupervised?"

Damon's confusion and annoyance must have shown on his face because Lionel cleared his throat and interjected. "What Brian means is that we didn't know who you were, or what you were doing here. We had to be safe, so we needed to have someone with eyes on you at all times. He motioned to Ike. "Ike here has been watching you from the skies almost since you got to the island."

Damon began to feel his blood rising. He didn't like being watched, but also couldn't deny the logic in what they'd done. But he still didn't quite understand. "I thought the Dutchman steered everyone away from this place. What, did you think I was some kind of spy or something?"

The room went silent, and Damon puzzled on whether he'd actually hit on something.

Lionel broke the silence when he said: "It was... a possibility."

"A spy for who?"

They all looked at one another. "We don't know, but... maybe we should start at the beginning." Lionel motioned for Damon to take a seat.

Brian started. "We're not the only... fairy tales... out here."

"No?" Asked Damon, sitting himself into a chair beside Lionel. "Where's the rest?"

"The Black Forest." answered Brian. "You've probably heard of it."

Heard of it? I grew up there. "Ya..." he said, his mind starting to wander. *Should I tell them?* "So, who's out there? Little Bo Peep? Maybe a long-lost son of Robin Hood?"

The room went silent. "We don't actually know," said Lionel. "But, the long-lost *great-grandson* of Robin Hood is actually here with us, you met him already."

I did? "Right." he said. "I remember." He didn't.

Lionel continued. "We all used to be from that forest, at least in the beginning. But there we're a handful that drove our ancestors out of that forest. Jacob Grimm turned this island into a haven for the survivors."

Damon raised an eyebrow. "So, why not take it back?"

Brian thumped a hand on the table. "We have. Three separate generations, three times over."

"And?" Damon asked, although he already knew the answer.

Lionel looked at him nervously. "You had asked a few times why there were no adults on the island. Well... Our numbers have been dwindling in the past fifty years, and they decided that they would make a last-ditch effort to reclaim the Black Forest. And..." Lionel got choked up.

"And they never came back." Damon finished for him.

Lionel nodded, tears welling in his eyes.

"Have you ever thought to go looking for them?"

"We wanted to." It was Brian speaking again. "But they took the last of the boats. As far as we're concerned: we're stranded."

"Until now." Ike gave Damon a smile.

Damon was confused. "Do you have someone here who can turn into a boat or something?"

Ike rolled his eyes. "No, your boat. The one you came in on. Something must be wrong with their navigation ever since the dutchman attacked, because they're still sailing close to the island."

That make Damon guffaw. "It's not my boat, it's the Admiral's, Admiral Wolf Carley, and trust me: he is *not* letting you borrow it.

Monty grinned. "No one said anything about *borrowing*."

"And just how do you expect to go about "not borrowing" this ship from the Admiral?"

Brian looked at Monty, annoyed. "Well, if Monty gets his way, we go in for death or glory. But I was hoping we could simply pay for it."

"Pay for it? Even if you could bring the ship to shore, do you know how much the Blacktooth is worth? It's not even Wolf's to sell!" He paused. "How do you even have money? You obviously got a lot of this stuff from the mainland."

Brian smirked and nodded to Astor, who took off one of his white linen gloves. As he picked up one of the euros that Damon had left on the table, Damon was shocked to see it turn to gold before his very eyes. Brian saw the flicker in Damon's eye.

"Astor is the great-great-something grandson of King Midas," he explained. "Those of us that can pass for normal on the mainland take his gold into the cities. It gets us by."

Damon looked around at all the velvets and silks surrounding him. *That and then some.* Then it dawned on him "If you make trips to the mainland, it means you can take me there the next time you go."

Lionel frowned. "We haven't left the island in months. We told you that our parents left to return to the Black Forest, but they took our last few boats to do so."

"We're stranded," added Astor, as he slipped his glove back over his fingers.

"Only until they return for us," piped in Lionel. Though Brian gave him a look that said: *you should know better.*

Damon furrowed his brow. "What about the Dutchman's ship?"

"Only if you're dead, that's the only way to sail that ship." Brian rose to his feet. You're stuck with us now, Grimm."

Lionel shrugged. "Maybe it was fate. You're Damon *Grimm.* There has to be something in that, right?"

Damon didn't answer.

✳ ✳ ✳

When Damon got back to his room in the tower, it was almost morning, and he was exhausted. Not bothering to change into more comfortable clothes, he flopped face-first onto the mattress. Just seconds later there was a knock at the door. Damon groaned into the bedding. *Who is it now...?*

"Come in... I guess." His voice was muffled. Damon heard the door creak open, and rolled onto his back.

"Hi," said Briar, as she shut the door behind her. She was wearing red, as always, in the form of a nightgown. She wasn't wearing a bra, and Damon could see the outline of her nipples beneath the cloth. Damon blinked twice to make sure it wasn't a dream. He tried to think of something to say

"Um... I thought you'd have been at the meeting?"

She smiled her same coy smile and gave Damon a little head tilt. "I had to get ready." Damon's eyes widened as she dropped her gown to the floor. She was naked beneath.

"Oh."

She giggled and walked over to him. "Is that all you have to say?"

He looked past her at the door. "Does it have a lock?"

She grinned, and straddled him where he lay, placing a hand on his chest. "Nope." She kissed him on the lips.

"Your brother - "

Briar rolled her eyes. "Please *do not* make me think of my brother right now." She pulled the shirt from up over Damon's head. "Now are you gonna' do me, or not?

Damon and Briar went well into the morning. Although, it was so close to morning already that it wasn't saying much. Damon had assumed she'd leave after they'd finished, but instead she snuggled up next to him and closed her eyes. Damon had wrapped an arm around her, and that's how they'd slept. As Damon awoke, and found her still sleeping naked beside him, he smiled. He'd never had many... *encounters* before. That's not to say he was a virgin. Just... inexperienced. Briar didn't seem to notice though. She wasn't too well versed either, living on an island and all.

The door suddenly burst open, and Ike scampered in. "Damon, the Blacktooth is nearing the island. We have to act now. Brian is waiting - " He stopped and stared.

Briar yawned and opened her eyes. Then she sat up startled and covered her breasts. "Ike..?"

Fuck.

CHAPTER 09

Brian stood by the longtable in Grimmhaven's mess hall with Notty on his right and Monty on his left. As Woody led Damon into the hall, it felt much colder than it had before. He noticed that Brian was anxiously fingering at the hilt of his blade. *Probably itching to cut my head off.* When he looked around, he noticed Ike was off to one side, looking uncomfortable and trying to not look Damon in the eye. *Little snitch.* After he'd found Damon with Briar, Ike had wasted no time charging downstairs to tell Brian. Damon barely had time to dress before Woody barged in to escort Damon downstairs. At least now the kid had the decency to look ashamed.

Woody led Damon until he was uncomfortably close to Brian. So close that he could smell the ham on Brian's breath. Brian stared at him, unblinking. There was a certain fire behind those eyes that reminded Damon of an angry father.

"I only have one question for you, Damon: did you do it?"

Damon smirked. "Twice."

Brian frowned. In one swift motion, he drew his ornate sword from his red leather scabbard and swung it in front of Damon's face. Before he could react, steel touched flesh, and Damon felt a sting across his left cheek. His head whipped around and a few drops of blood spattered against the ground. Damon scowled, and whipped back around, looking to scatter Brian's teeth across the floor. He paused though, when he saw the tip of the sword pointed inches from his eye. Damon raised his hands in a show of surrender, while a trickle on blood streamed down his cheek.

"Damon Grimm," Brian almost spit out the words. "I challenge you to a duel."

"A duel?" Damon batted the sword away with the back of his hand. "My god, what century do you think this is?"

Brian grit his teeth and took another swing, but this time Damon was ready. Stepping forward, he caught Brian's arm with his one hand, and knocked him back onto his ass with the other. His sword escaped his grasp and went clattering across the stone floor. Both Notty and Monty made to grab Damon, but Brian gave them a motion not to. Groaned, he propped himself back up to his knees, but landed square on his back when Damon kicked him in the chest.

I shouldn't do this, Damon thought. But he was angry and needed a good fight. Flashbacks of his first time as a navyman filled his head, and his right hand began to throb. Brian coughed, and again tried to get back up. But before he could, Damon was on him. Straddling his chest, Damon landed blow after blow to Brian's face until his right eye had swelled to a deep purple. Notty had seen enough. He grabbed Damon by the arm and attempted to pull him off. Damon was having none of it. He pulled back, and Notty stumbled, tripping over Brian where he lay and landing hard on his shoulder.

Brian spit at him and made an attempt to grab Damon by his hair. Damon batted his hand away and placed a hand firmly around Brian's throat.

"ENOUGH!"

Briar Rose pushed through the amassing crowd of onlookers to where the two were. She was wearing the same flowing red dress that Damon had first met her in. He could see that she had tears welling in her eyes as she gave Damon a shove.

"Get *OFF*!"

Her push barely moved him, but her words did more. Sheepishly, Damon rose to his feet. Briar gave him another shove for good measure, then dropped to her knees and cradled her brother's head. Brian gently waved her away, but she didn't go. Still, he rose on his own, picking his sword with one hand while wiping blood from his nose with the other. Damon was ready for him to take another swing at him, but he never did. Instead, he walked over to the nearest chair and sat. Damon forced his body to relax. His cheek was still bleeding, and so his placed his palm on it, grimacing at the sting.

It only then occurred to Damon that everyone was staring at him. He hadn't even noticed it before, but most if not everyone on the island was in the mess hall. And now, they all looked horrified.

It was Lionel who ended up breaking the silence. Clearing his throat to take people's attention of Brian as Briar attended to his wound. "There was a reason to bring you all here, but it wasn't for... this." He winced. "As you are all aware, we have had no means of getting to the mainland since our parents' voyage. Most of you probably know that Damon came here by boat. A very big one at that." He motioned to Ike and the boy came forward.

"Last night... on my flight around the island. I saw it. The ship is coming so close to the shore we have a chance."

"A chance for what, exactly?" Nelda asked.

Damon answered when Ike did not "To take the ship, and use it to sail to the mainland. To find out what happened to your parents."

One of the Chinese brothers scrunched his face up in utter shock. "*Take* the ship!?"

Another of the triplets continued the thought. "And even if we somehow do that, we already know what happened to our parents."

The third finished. "The same thing that's happened to all of us who have ever gone into the Black Forest.

"They never come back!" the three said in unison.

Damon thought about it for a moment before saying: "I have."

That got everyone's attention, even Briar's. "What do you mean?" she asked.

"I was born there. In a small hamlet right in the middle of the forest. I got lost in those woods as a child, but *something* led me out.

"What was it?" asked Ike, intrigued.

Damon shrugged. "I would tell you if I knew. But the important part is this: I think that I could help you get that ship, and then help you get into that forest. My parent's old house was abandoned. I bet when the other's tried to enter, they didn't have a place to regroup."

A few heads nodded agreement, but more still were looking at Damon with scepticism and anger.

A man standing beside Nikki that Damon did not know spoke up. "Once we get there, are you going to beat us like you did Brian?" A few shouts of agreement followed.

Damon bit his lip. "No... and... I'm sorry." He looked towards Brian. "I'm sorry." Brian didn't look back. Damon continued. "I'm not the best person for this, but I'm what you've got right now. I know the crew of this ship; I know the Admiral. I know the Black Forest. I'm sorry, but if you want to try and find out what happened to your parents, you're going to have to trust me on this."

Moments passed. So many moments that Damon was worried that no one would agree with him. But after a pause, Lionel moved over beside him.

"Damon is not perfect, but I think we have to trust him to do this. I want to try."

Theodore was still on his shoulder, and nodded his agreement.

Ike stepped forward. "I know where the ship is going to be, I can guide you to it."

A few others nodded agreement and pledged to come along. Nikki was next, then Charlotte. Then a boy named Tyler Hood, who Damon barely knew and was more than a little surprised to have on his side. Astor came next, saying that they might still be able to buy the Admiral's ship with his gold. Damon was still doubtful, but agreed to try. Last was Marlin. Zack attempted to come once Marlin had offered, but the older boy shut that down right away.

Damon nodded. *Nine may be enough, if all goes well.* He turned to Brian. "We need to make our move now. The ship is due to pass in less than a day." Brian didn't look up at him. Damon moved closer. "Brian, you're the leader here, not me. I need you in on this for it to work."

"Go to hell, Damon."

He ignored that. "Brian, don't you want to save your people?"

Brian threw his sword to the ground, causing Briar to leap back. "Not if I have to save them with you!"

Brian turned, and stormed from the hall, leaving everyone in a stunned silence. He paused at the door and looked back, pointing a finger at Damon.

"If you get anyone else hurt Damon, I'll make sure you never step foot in Grimmhaven again." He slammed the big entrance door behind him, sending an echo through the mess hall. Briar gave one last look to Damon before trailing after him. Damon's injured hand throbbed like never before. He sighed.

He was surprised as someone gripped him by the arm. It was Notty. Damon Looked at him, confused, and perhaps ready to fight. But Notty didn't look like he was about to throw a punch, so Damon allowed himself to relax. "What is it?"

Notty shrugged. "Come with me."

Damon followed Notty back down into the dungeons. Gruff was snoring in his cell. Damon gave Notty a puzzled look.

"Those bunch you're bringing, they've got a good heart, but none of them are worth anything if things go... *sour* out there. He unlocked the door with a clank. The sound made Gruff snort awake. Notty took a big breath. "If things go bad... make sure he's on your side."

"Why don't you just come with us?" Damon asked. "We could use you."

Notty shook his head. "No, my place is here." He thought for a moment, then took his World War Two era revolver out of its holster and handed it handle-first to Damon. "Just in case."

* * *

"Remember," Damon cautioned as the group stood on the windswept rocky shoreline. "We aren't here to fight them; we only need to commandeer the ship. If we can, we'll buy the ship from them. It could all go smooth." But even as the words left his mouth, he was already doubting their validity.

Lionel was crouching beside him, his orange fur matted with sweat. Damon put a hand on his friend's shoulder. Lionel looked up and gave a half-hearted smile. He looked much more human than beast in the first light of the sun. From above, Damon watched as a grey feathered arrow arced across the sky. That was the signal from Tyler. Damon nodded towards Nikki. The pale girl was even whiter than usual today. Composing herself, she walked forwards towards the shoreline. She was barefoot, and the gravel shifted beneath her feet as she moved. As she reached the water's edge, she knelt, and slid her hands beneath the water's surface. She paused a moment, taking a deep breath, then flexed her fingers. Frost began to pepper the surface of the water. Within a few minutes, a thin layer of ice could be seen stretching into the distance.

* * *

"Admiral!" The call came from behind him. Admiral Wolf Carley turned around to find one of his men with sweat on his brow and a look of death of his face. All colour was drained from the man's cheeks.

"Shtatus?" Admiral Wolf growled.

The man could barely get the words out. "It's the readings," he started. "The water around the island... something's wrong."

Wolf grimaced. "Be shpecific, boy."

"Ice!" He exclaimed, obviously not sure how to properly explain it. "The island is surrounded by *ice*! You don't think–"

"–that it'sh the curse?" Wolf interrupted. "No, I don't." He turned and returned to staring out over the railing, a black gloved hand gripped tightly on the hilt of his cutlass, his sideburns furrowed. "Back to your post, boy."

He saluted and scampered off.

✳ ✳ ✳

Damon waited anxiously on the shoreline. Tyler was supposed to give another signal when they had turned the ship towards shore. Nikki was already quavering at the water's edge, the energy all but gone from her. *We don't have much time left to do this.* Damon looked up to where Ike perched himself on a rock, legs close to his chest, and his wings tucked behind him.

"Ike." Damon called. The boy turned. "Go see what's up."

Ike nodded. He took the googles from off his head and placed them over his eyes. Leaping from the rock, he free-fell for a moment, before giving a flap of his wings. He soared off towards the tower where Tyler was watching. Damon had to cover his eyes as he went, as Ike became a spec in the sky. The spec landed atop the stone tower, and disappeared momentarily, before returning in a swooping arc. His wings kicked up a waft of sand as he landed back on the ground, removing his goggles.

"Well?" asked Damon, squinting from the puff of sand.

"They aren't stopping. Look's like if anything they're speeding up."

Damon grimaced. Nikki sat exhausted on the shoreline, no longer freezing the waters. It would do no good to push her harder. Damon wracked his brain. "And no sign of the Dutchman?" Ike shook his head.

Damon furrowed his brow, and looked to the men and women around him. Something gave him an idea.

"Marlin!" He called. The tall boy looked up from where he knelt next to Nikki, adjusting his glasses.

"Yes, Damon?" The boy looked as though he thought Damon might hurt him."

Damon crossed his arms. "How well can you conjure lightning?"

***

Admiral Wolf stood at the prow of his ship, peering over the railing. Below, the ship was cutting into chunks of ice. They were thin, but still enough to leave scratches in the hull. Much longer, and those scratches would turn to gouges. His ship was strong, he knew, but she wasn't cut out for ice water. He turned to call an order to his helmsman, but before he could, the hairs on his cheeks stood on end. He gripped back the railing, but a zap of static hit him from the metal, even through his gloves. Wolf clenched his hand and brought it back up to his chest. He could smell the electricity in the air. Suddenly, a bright flash lit up the sky, and an arc of blinding light shot from the sky in the direction of the island. The light forked, and one of the tongs struck the deck not twenty meters from where Wolf stood. He leapt nearly three feet in the air as the deck shook below him. A sailor grabbed him by the arm.

"Fire, Admiral, FIRE!"

Fire? *Fire on what*? Wolf was confused. But as he looked around from where he lay, he saw it; a billow of fire ripped the sky from the wood from where the lightning had hit. He leapt to his feet. His side ached from where he'd hit the deck. He tore the cutlass from his scabbard and started pointed it at his mates.

"Water!" he called to one. "Extinguisher!" to another. The sailors ran around like chickens with their heads cut off, this way and that, trying desperately to quell the flames. In the chaos, Wolf felt someone grab his arm. He nearly cut the man down in the confusion, but stopped when he saw it was one of his own men.

"The ship is taking too much damage!" he yelled. "We need to dock. Now!"

✳ ✳ ✳

Damon breathed a sigh of relief as he watched the ship come over the horizon. They weren't out of the woods just yet. Getting the ship to dock on the island was the easy part, and the safest. Now they had to take the ship... and hope to not get anyone hurt in doing so.

CHAPTER 10

Astor was the one to walk out with Damon. Damon still had hopes that it might be possible to simply *buy* the ship with enough gold. But deep down, he knew that Admiral Wolf would never go for it. Despite it being salt stained and torn, Damon thought it fitting to wear his uniform as he approached the ship, docked and smoking by the treeline. He'd placed Tyler in the trees as extra cover for them. Ike was also nearby, circling in the sky. At the height he was at, he looked no different than a large bird to the average observer. Anyone who cared to watch him for a while would notice the difference soon enough, though. He hoped that would not happen.

Nikki and Marlin had pushed the limits of their powers too much though, and had stayed back by the rocks. The rest of the group: Lionel, Theodore, Charlotte, and Gruff, were nearby, just out of sight. But with the crew already thinking the island was cursed, he figured it wouldn't be a good idea to have them being seen. Not yet, at least

Astor looked concerned. He carried a small bag of golden trinkets in a burlap sack, and was currently shifted the bag nervously from one hand to the other. "So, what's this Wolf guy like."

"You'll see soon enough." Damon moved one hand to the revolver in his waistband, loosening it slightly. "Just don't get too comfortable until its over."

Astor nodded. He took a look into the burlap sack he carried. Inside, solid gold coins, cups, shells, and other trinkets jangled against each other. "Do you think we need more?"

No. Damon thought. "Sure," he said. "Anything might help."

Astor took off a glove and began scooping up stones off the beach. They were grey when he picked them off the ground, but gold as they dropped from his fingers into the sack. *I'll never get used to that,* thought Damon.

It only took them another few minutes of walking before the first crewman noticed them. The man yelled out, and suddenly there were near twenty men by the railing. Half of them with gun's drawn. Astor had drastically slowed his pace. A bead of sweat rolling down the side of his face. Damon put a hand on his shoulder and gave him a nod. The sand at their feet exploded as the CRACK of a shot rang out. Astor dropped instinctively to the ground, the sack opening and spraying golden trinkets along the beach, strewn amongst the sand. The golden-haired boy scampered off closer to the treeline. Damon's hand went for his own revolver when he heard a familiar voice call out from up on deck.

"SHEIZE FIRE!"

Damon looked up to see Admiral Wolf Carley, hand as ever on the hit of his cutlass, staring down at him.

"It's Dexter!" he heard someone yell. And just like that, all hands were on deck, all to see the man they had tossed from their ship. Brocksmith at least had the decency to look ashamed.

Astor looked up at him from where he was lying. "Dexter?"

Damon smirked, and met the crewman's gaze. "It's Damon, actually. Damon Grimm."

That sent a few puzzled murmurs amongst the crew.

Astor had found his courage again, and was collecting the golden items back into his sack. A few of the crewman were whispering to one another. Probably about: *who is he*, or: *is that real gold?* Damon thought.

Wolf was looking down at him, uninterested in Astor or his gold. *That doesn't bode well.* Damon thought.

"Come aboard... Damon." The Admiral made a motion with his hand and the ramp was lowered. Damon nervously began up the steps. Astor followed close behind, knuckles white from gripping the sack of gold so tight. Wolf laid a fat paw of a hand on Damon's chest as he reached the deck, then grabbed his collar and pulled him closer. Damon could smell whiskey layering the already stale breath wafting from the Admiral's mouth.

"You're shuposed to be dead."

"I guess you didn't try hard enough."

Wolf grinned. "Everyone back to your shtations!" he yelled, releasing Damon's collar. "Damon, my quarters. And bring that shorry excuse for a man with you."

Astor pointed to himself and Damon gave him a reassuring shrug. Around them, the men returned to repairing the ship. Brocksmith made an attempt to get Damon's attention, but Damon only looked away hottedly. As they walked to the captain's quarters. Damon heard a *THUNK* from atop the roof, and Ike peered down from his perch. Damon motioned for him to stay out of sight while they went inside. Astor didn't even seem to notice.

Inside the Captain's quarters, Damon reached out a hand and motioned for Astor to pass him the sack of gold. The golden-haired boy did, and Damon turned the sack upside down, emptying the contents haphazardly onto Wolf's table, and letting little golden things bounce off and get strewn across the cabin floor. Wolf was unamused.

"You beached my ship," he said simply.

Damon raised an eyebrow. "You threw me off your ship."

"You were dishonerably dishcharged."

So, you did know the whole time. "And yet you still brought me aboard."

"You had a falsh name."

Damon scoffed "Like you didn't know who I was."

That made Wolf smirk. "Why are you trying to get back onboard. Mish me?"

Damon motioned to the gold strewn about. "As you might have guessed, I came to buy your ship."

That actually made Wolf laugh. "Government's ship. I only sail it."

"Good," said Damon. "Then the payday is all that much bigger."

"You're a little rat is what you are."

Damon never thought that Wolf would go for the money, but now it was obvious. He knew he had to change gears.

"Take the gold Wolf, we're taking this ship one way or another."

"Who's taking my ship? By *we* do you mean you and that prishy-boy?" He gave a snarling expression to Astor. "And it's *Admiral* to you, *worm*. You two need my ship? For what? Weekend getaway for two?"

Damon scoffed. "You stopped being my admiral when you threw me overboard. You have no idea what's this island is, and what you have coming if you don't surrender the ship right now." Damon tensed his jaw. He knew he was pushing it at this point.

The Admiral stared at him for a moment, then to Astor, then back at Damon. "You think I have no idea?"

Wolf drew the cutlass from his belt. Astor shrieked, and Damon made a move for his gun, but it snagged on his jacket as he tried to pull it out. As the Admiral moved forward with surprising speed, Damon moved back. But he tripped, and landed hard on his ass. Wolf stood over him, ready to strike. There was only a single small porthole in the captain's chambers, but through it came a grey feathered arrow that thrummed as it struck Wolf in the hand, cutlass falling to the ground as a roar of pain escaped his lips.

Damon took no time before capitalizing on the situation. Reaching forward, he grabbed a golden goblin that had bounced to the ground from the sack. Damon wound back, and struck it across the Admiral's brow as hard as he could. The burly man went to one knee, but it wasn't enough to knock him out.

"Bashtard!" Wolf grimaced, blood trickling from his forehead and down over one eye.

Damon heard a sudden burst of gunshot from outside. He and Astor looked at one another with concern. Damon turned, and threw the door to the Admiral's quarter's open. Astor followed and the two of them rushed up on deck. When they rounded the corner, they could see three crewman pointing rifles over the railing at the treeline. One was trembling, and he sent another few rounds at the ground below.

"DEMON!" the crewman yelled. "I saw it! It's over there!"

Another burst exploded from his gun into the treeline. Without thinking, Damon charged the man from behind and tackled him to the ground. The other crew stared stunned for a moment, before turning their own weapons on him.

"Get off him, Dexter," said one of the men, pointing his assault rifle at Damon.

Damon rolled off and put up his hands. He noticed one of the men was Fritz, the man he played cards with before all this had started.

"How did you live!?" Fritz demanded, in little more than a squeak. Damon could see the confusion and terror in his eyes. "Who... who's out there? Are they with you? *What* is out here with you?"

A dark shadow passed overhead, and Ike gave a sold kick to Fritz's head as he flew past. The force sent the rifle spiralling from the man's hand, as he stumbled back to the railing, where he flipped over the side and splashed down into the shallow water below. A second shadow was crawling over the railing on the opposite side of the ship. Within moments, both of the other crewmen were down on the ground, a net of thick webbing covering them. The shadow's aim wasn't so good though, and Damon found himself stuck to the ground as well.

"Sorry." Charlotte apologized as she came over, using one of her sharp arachnid legs to cut him free. One of the men screamed like a banshee at the sight of her. Charlotte looked pained at that. She spun a small web and stuck it not-so-lightly over the man's mouth.

Damon stood. "There's no chance of negotiations now. We have to take the ship by force."

Ike landed beside them. "What about the crew?"

Damon shrugged. "Grimmhaven has a dungeon, doesn't it? It's comfortable enough for them to stay until the rest of us get back. And Nelda and a few others can stay behind to look after them for a week or so." He wasn't thrilled at the idea, but it was the best option they had. Although, the thought of throwing Admiral Carley in a cage like an animal pleased him more than he cared to admit.

Despite the commotion, the majority of the crew were still working on ship repairs on the other end of the ship. But shouts of a demon had started to bring a few closer to come see what was happening. Not a lot, but more than Damon was comfortable with. He picked up a rifle off of one of the men on the ground. Damon motioned for the others to do the same. Ike refused.

"I can't hold that and fly at the same time."

Damon nodded. Astor also looked like he wanted to refuse. "Take it." Damon shoved the gun in front of the boy. "It's only to defend ourselves. We don't shoot unless they do first."

Astor took it, but sheepishly. Damon knew he'd be no good in a firefight if worse came to worse, but he wanted the boy armed none-theless. From up the ramp walked Gruff, dressed in heavy iron plate from shoulder to foot and resting what Lionel had told him was his father's warhammer on one shoulder. Lionel himself followed, with Theodore Thumb on his shoulder.

"Fuckers called me a demon." Gruff seemed more than a little annoyed. But Damon couldn't deny that he would have thought

the same seeing a seven-foot-tall black goat. Astor gave him a little
shrug, obviously thinking the same thing.

Ike was watching anxiously as more of the crew began to move
closer to them. "What should we do, Damon?"

All the other's looked to him. If he was leader only by default
before, that was no longer the case. He needed a plan, and fast.
Damon looked around to all of them "Lionel and Gruff, you two
keep the crew at bay. Try to distract them while Charlotte inca-
pacitates them with her web. Ike, you make sure no one sneaks up
anyone." Ike nodded and jumped off the edge of the boat, Damon
watched as he soared off into the sky.

"Astor." The boy looked to him nervously. "You're with me. I'm
not leaving the Admiral where we can't see him."

Theodore Thumb looked hurt. "And me?"

Damon gave him an apologetic smile. "Stay here, Theo," Damon
checked the rifle he held in his hands. "Unless you can figure out a
way to carry one of these."

* * *

When Damon and Astor returned to the Admiral's quarters,
Wolf Carley was nowhere to be found; only a trail of blood leading
from the doorway, and two halves of an arrow laying on the floor.

"Fuck!" Damon yelled as he kicked a golden cup against the wall.

Astor looked around nervously, as if Wolf were about to jump
out at them from some corner.

"Come on," said Damon. "We need to find him."

As Damon was about to grab the door handle, it swung open and
knocked Damon backwards. His rifle was thrown from his grip and
he saw stars for a few seconds. Astor panicked and pointed his rifle
in the direction of the door. Damon stumbled, but rubbed his head,
and motioned for Astor to move to the other end of the room. He
did, but not before two navymen entered in a fluster. One grabbed

the rifle from Astor's hands and threw it across the room. The other pinned Damon against the wall.

Astor grabbed a candlestick off the Admiral's desk and swung it at the first man, but it glanced off his shoulder. Angered, the navyman swung back, his fist catching Astor on the cheek. Damon threw his assailant backwards, and grabbed Notty's revolver from his waistband. Damon's fingers trembled, trying to cock it, but he was still dazed and kept missing. The navymen had found their fingers, however, and both reached for their own guns. Damon hadn't gotten a good look at either of them, but one looked familiar with his shaggy black hair and goatee.

The shaggy haired sailor fired at Astor; his body completely exposed. He missed, but only barely. Astor bull rushed him, slamming both of them to the ground. Damon had finally cocked his pistol, and kicked down the Admiral's desk in hopes to use it as cover. But he soon realized how futile that was as two bullets exploded through the wood next to him. From where he lay struggling, Astor noticed as well. In one motion, he yanked a thick leather glove off his left hand and grabbed a table leg. Rapidly expanding out from his touch, the oak turned yellow, then shined with the gleam of solid 24 karat gold. Two more shots came down, but deflected harmlessly off the metal surface.

The next shot struck, however, as the man took aim at Astor. The bullet pierced the golden-haired teen in the side, just below the ribs.

Astor cried out. The shaggy sailor took the opportunity and straddled Astor as he bled, aiming his pistol at his face. Astor panicked, and instinctively grabbed the gun. From his touch it turned solid, and when the sailor tried to pull the trigger it would not budge.

"Shit!" he cried as he threw it to the side. He made a move to punch Astor, but Astor grabbed his wrist as he did. The skin down to the hand began to become mottled as it transmuted. The gold ran like an infection, spreading all the way up just before the terrified sailor's elbow before he screamed. Astor seemed to realize what he was doing at that moment and let go. The sailor fell backwards with a *THUNK*. His left hand gripping his now solid right arm, hand clenched in an eternal metal fist. The other sailor stood stunned in the doorway; pistol pointed to the ground. He never noticed Damon as he trod up to him, the handle of his revolving knocking hard against his temple as he fell to the floor.

Now that Damon had a good look, he could see the shaggy haired sailor was Kent, a nice boy who liked to play cards in the mess room. Now, the boy lay mouth agape. Damon couldn't tell if the arm was too heavy to lift, or if he was too scared to try. His attention then quickly shifted to Astor. The teen lay next to Kent, holding his side. Astor's powers didn't work on himself, so the wound stayed fleshy at his touch.

Damon knelt beside Astor, tearing a strip off his own shirt and binding it around the boy's chest. Astor screamed and writhed on the floor. Damon had to dodge the boy's twitching fingers, lest they graze against his skin. Every time he moved, blood welled and ran, the cloth could not stop the flow. Damon had to act fast. Reaching down, he pulled off a shoe, and dumped the sand into the wound, enough to fill the hole and then some. Astor screamed again. Damon then caught the boy's hand where it flailed, and pressed the palm against the wound. Blood trickled between his fingers at first, but soon stopped. When Damon pulled the hand away, there was a golden plug in Astor's side. It was crude, and would probably need proper treatment afterwards. But for now, he was stable.

Damon heard muttering in the corner of the room, turning his head, he saw Kent staring horrified at his arm. He'd backed himself into the corner of the room, sitting knees to his chest hyperventilating, his left hand holding up his right, like it was too heavy to lift on its own. Damon stood before him, pity in his eyes. A wave of anger and confusion seemed to wash over the sailor. He leapt to his feet and made a clumsy swing at Damon with his golden hand. But the weight was all wrong for the punch, and Damon needed only to lazily move to the side as the man sprawled face first onto the floor.

The pity was gone from Damon. Kneeling, he grabbed Kent by the scruff of his shirt and brought him to his face.

"Where is Wolf?" He asked bluntly.

Kent couldn't find his tongue, but didn't need to. Damon felt a leather glove on his shoulder throw him to the side as he went careening into the wall. *Always was a strong man*, he mused. Wolf had the look of an angered animal, his shirt was ripped in the front, and puffs of thick black chest hair heaved with every breath.

"Grimm!" he yelled, and ran headlong towards Damon. "Grimm!"

Damon had to roll to the side to get out of the way, nearly tripping on Astor as he did. Wolf's right glove was crusted with dried blood, and as the Admiral's heart began pumping faster, fresh blood began to drip from the wound. Wolf's cutlass still lay on the floor where he had dropped it before. Damon made a move to grab it, but that only seemed to anger Wolf more. As Damon bent over and reached down, a bony knee hit him in the chest, knocking the wind from his lungs.

He stumbled, and tried to steady himself on the Admiral's overturned golden desk, but couldn't catch his breath. Damon gasped, wheezed and coughed. Wolf grinned, and kicked the desk, making Damon lose his balance and fall to the floor.

From where he lay sprawled, he watched a large spider crawl in through the door and smiled. Eight limbs were suddenly wrapped around Wolf like a backpack. Confused, the Admiral turned, only to have Lionel give him a swipe across the cheek with a paw. Charlotte weaved a web with two of her legs, and slung it across Wolf's chest, still clinging to his back. Theo stuck him through the foot with his needle-sword, and Wolf dropped to one knee. The Admiral gave one last roar before Charlotte wrapped a line of silk about his mouth. Damon rose and thanked them. Only then did any of them notice Astor. It was Lionel who did first, as he dropped to one knee beside his passed-out friend.

"No..." he whispered, tail drooping.

"He's alive," Damon reassured him. "But we need to get him back to Grimmhaven."

Lionel nodded. Damon very gently put Astor's glove back over his hand. Then, the two of them carried Astor up the stairs to the deck.

"What about him?" Theo pointed to where the Admiral knelt on the floor, body covered in silk, eyes filled with rage.

Damon thought about it for a moment. "We'll come back for him after. We take care of our own first."

Theo nodded, and Charlotte lowered a hand so he could climb on. The four of them climbed back on deck. Damon was surprised to see that the rest of the crew had been tied up by Charlotte. He was about to congratulate the others for their job when Ike landed in front of them with a worried expression on his face.

"Guys." He was breathing hard, a sense of urgency in his eyes. "We have a problem."

CHAPTER 11

Gruff stood over the crewman, warhammer at the ready. The man lay with one arm held in front of him in a futile attempt to stop what he knew was coming. The other was crumpled on his chest, forearm purple and shattered.

"Please." he sputtered as blood ran run down the corner of his mouth. "Please."

"That's enough, Gruff!" Damon pulled the revolver from his waistband and pointed it at his ally.

"Demon!" Gruff pointed a hairy finger with a jagged nail at the injured man where he lay bleeding. "Called me... a *demon!*"

Damon could see the rage flicker in Gruff's eyes and for a moment, he wondered if he would have to put the beast down.

"We aren't here to execute the crew. We have Admiral Wolf. we've taken the ship, you can stop!"

Gruff gave a roar, and smashed his Warhammer down next to the man's head and let it stick there. The man gave a yelp as the wood cracked, but it was a weak one, almost a whimper. Gruff then turned to Damon, and raised his arms, as if to taunt him into taking the shot. Damon only shook his head, and tried to look as authoritatively as he could. A look that was meant to meant *calm down.*

Gruff met Damon's gaze, but then looked past it. "You!" He cried, yanking the warhammer from its place embedded in the smashed deck.

In unison, Damon and the others whirled around to find Admiral Wolf standing behind them. Over one shoulder he carried a harpoon gun.

Shit. Damon thought. He fired, but the gun was old, and it misfired. Damon felt the sting of the heat on his hand and dropped the weapon to the deck. *I'm lucky it didn't blow up in my hand.* He heard a roar from behind him and Damon turned to see Gruff charge headlong at the Admiral, raising his warhammer high into the air, glinting the sun's light off it's silver finish.

Damon wanted to scream for Gruff to stop, but he knew if wouldn't work. So, he hesitated. It was only for a moment, but it was enough. Wolf aimed, pulled the trigger, and a harpoon a meter long cut the salt sea air over the deck. Gruff didn't flinch at the sight of the pike coming towards him. But the plate armour he wore was old, and brittle, and the modern steel cut through it like butter. Gruff stopped in his tracks, hoofs stumbling against the deck. A foot and a half of steel protruded from his chest. Wide-eyed, Damon watched as the goat-man stumbled left, then right, then was gone off the edge of the Blacktooth.

Damon silently raged for a moment as he watched Wolf grin from where he stood. He wanted to go take him to the ground, to wipe that smile off his face. But he didn't. Instead, Damon dove from the railing, down twenty feet into the water below. Lionel and Charlotte had both jumped in with him.

Damon felt cold water fill his nose and mouth. The water was shallow, maybe only fifteen feet to the bottom. Damon easily touched it on the way down. It was murky, and the water stung his eyes, but Damon forced himself to keep them open. He saw a sting of red float by him, and moved his gaze to where it came from. He saw Lionel and Charlotte already at the body, heaving to lift Gruff to the surface. But Guff was near 400 pounds, and covered in heavy plate. And besides all that: he was already dead.

Damon surfaced, gasping for breath, when a harpoon struck the water inches from him. In response, he gasped, and nearly sucked in a mouthful of water. Charlotte and Lionel had also surfaced, and the three of them looked like sitting ducks in the water. Wolf was at the railing, already having reloaded his weapon. He held it in one hand, with the other holding Theodore in a tight grip. The small man struggled, but that only made Wolf squeeze tighter.

What the hell is Tyler doing? The Hood was supposed to take Wolf out at a time like this. He'd taken the shot before, and Damon knew he could take it now. Something must have happened, but he had no time to worry about that now.

"Thish... ish *MY* ship!" Admiral Wolf called down in his signature lisp. He pointed the harpoon gun towards Theodore. "Come up on deck now. All of you. Or he gets it."

Damon's heart skipped a beat. *Then it's over.* He began to swim towards the ramp, looking back and seeing that Lionel and Charlotte were doing the same. He mourned for Gruff, but right now he could only think about Theo. Just as they were reaching the ramp, a shadow came down over them again. Even Wolf seemed to notice it. Pausing, he looked up to the sky, and saw Ike flying straight towards him. Wolf turned his harpoon gun, but Ike did not flinch. Wolf fired, and the projectile struck Ike in the wing, in an explosion of wood and feathers. Ike lost control, but was still on course. With the full weight of his body, he struck the Admiral like a bowling ball and knocked him clean into the air, two feet up, and eight feet back.

Damon watched as Wolf, Ike, and Theodore rained down into the water. Lionel swam back over to help Theo; Charlotte did the same with Ike. It was Damon himself who went to get Wolf. The Admiral was sopping wet when Damon came upon him.

"Nicsh move." Wolf coughed and winced in pain as he tried to stay afloat. Damon judged that more than a few of his ribs were broken from Ike's impact.

Damon grabbed him hard by the collar. "You're coming with me, *Admiral*. He spit the rank at him. He was tired of the games. Wolf surprisingly, did not protest. Or perhaps he was simply too weak to.

All of them returned to shore cold and wet. The first thing Damon did was wrap a cloth around Wolf's wrists, and then touch it to Astor's fingers. Even unconscious, everything he touched still turned to gold. Damon knew that the metal was soft, and that iron shackles would be better, but he was making due with what he had; and Charlottes webbing didn't seem to work. He put the admiral away from the rest of the crew and had Charlotte on permanent watch duty. Once Damon was satisfied, he went to check on the others.

It was only then that Damon noticed Lionel sitting on the beach nursing his ankle. Blood was trickling from where he had wrapped it in bandages. He was flicking smoothing small between his fingers, but stopped when Damon got closer.

"You're hurt." Damon said. It was more a statement than a question. Lionel shrugged and handed him the small object. Damon could see it was a small bullet. He rolled it around in his hand. "You got hit?" That time it *was* a question.

Lionel nodded. "Only a graze, I went and picked up the bullet after as a… memento." He laughed to himself. "It's silly, I know."

"No," Damon reassured him. "I would have done the same." He frowned. You're sure you're OK, though?"

Lionel nodded, and stood to show that he could put weight on it. Lionel's face showed that it still *did* hurt, but Damon decided not to call him on it. Instead, he squeezed Lionel's shoulder, and moved on to look at everyone else.

Theo was interestingly sitting alone for once. Normally, he was on Lionel's shoulder, or at very least nearby someone. But now he was sitting alone, staring out over the water. He didn't even seem no notice when Damon came near.

"Theo?" he asked.

"Hmmm?" Theo seemed to snap out of his trance. "What is it?"

"You were spaced out. You alright?"

"Oh, oh ya I'm fine." He stretched. "Hey, give me a lift, would you?"

Damon was surprisingly flattered to be asked. He knelt down and let the small man climb up onto his hand, then placed him on his shoulder. Theo gripped him by the shirt and they walked over to the others.

Ike was sitting beside Astor, who Damon was very happy to see had come to. Astor had his shirt off, and was picking at the golden plug in his side. Ike on the other hand, knelt crying over his wings.

"Ruined!" Ike yelled through tears. "I'll never fly again!" he punched again and again at the sand until his knuckles bled, then slumped over trembling, his wavy hair falling over his eyes as if to mask the tears streaking down his face.

Damon knelt beside him. "Are you sure we can't fix them. I'm sure the whole could be patched." Ike scowled at him, and Damon saw just how young Ike really was. "No!" He cried. "And even if you could, their soaked." He showed Damon a handful of dripping feathers. "That's one of *two* rules. Only *two*!"

"Is that the only pair of wings?" Ike nodded sadly.

Damon lowered his eyes, understanding. "I'm so sorry Ike. Just remember that you sacrificed your wings to save all of our lives. We wouldn't have made it without you."

After another few minutes of rest, Damon rallied everyone together; his men, and Wolf's. The sailors made thirty-two in total, which made Damon wonder what had happened to the rest since the Dutchman attack.

"That could have gone a lot worse," said Lionel to Damon.

"It could have gone a lot better, too." Damon turned to his friend. "Gruff died, Astor nearly died, you were shot, Ike is permanently grounded, and we still don't know what happened to Tyler." The boy had never regrouped with the rest. They hoped he was back at Grimmhaven, and had a good explanation for leaving when they needed him the most.

Charlotte had Wolf on a kind of spider-string leash. The Admiral coughed. "Off to the dungeons, then?" he asked, almost mockingly.

"Don't worry." Damon smirked. "They aren't as bad as they sound"

CHAPTER 12

When the small group returned to Grimmhaven, none looked like heroes. Damon led them; his cheek still scabby from where Brian had cut it. Lionel walked beside him, trying his best to not limp, but it was obvious to anyone who looked closely that he was favouring his right leg. The makeshift bandage wrapped about his ankle had been white when put on, but now it was pink. Nikki and Marlin each had an arm around Astor, who had taken a turn for the worse. As soon as Nelda saw him, she rushed over. Beckoning, a few of the others came round to help rush him down to her cabin. Theo rode on Charlotte's shoulder, and Ike carried his ruined wing pack. It was painfully obvious that Gruff was not with them.

Brian sat in the castle's crumbling throne, his sister beside him, holding a damp cloth against his cheek. The right half of his face was swollen and purple. He opened his good eye and glared down at the group. Nikki flicked her fingers and the damp cloth became frosted in ice. Brian seemed to enjoy that.

"Can I assume that this is the crew?" He asked, looking at the almost three dozen men standing nervously at the doorway.

Damon nodded. "I was hoping to put them... where you put me. At least until we return."

Brian nodded back. "Notty, Monty, Woody. You three take them down, make them comfortable."

The enforcers passed by Damon without speaking. Monty gave him a sneer, though. The ushered in the crewman past the hall and down the stairs. It was slow going, as they were bound at the wrists and ankles with webbing, and each was connected to the man behind him. As they entered, the crew began frantically looking around at the cacophony of faces surrounding them. One paused when seeing Elliot, with his huge elk horns and hooves. Noticing this, Elliot got right up in the man's face and gave him a look up and down. By Damon's estimation, the man nearly fainted where he stood.

The crewman that Gruff had nearly killed had a sling made of webbing around his arm, but his face was pale from blood loss and he nearly couldn't stand. Damon knew that they had to get him help soon. As soon as Nelda is done with Astor. *We take care of our own first.*

Wolf was last, Damon escorted him personally down to Gruff's old cell. The Admiral looked weaker than he had before, but Damon knew that he was still as dangerous as ever. Notty handed him the key, and Damon triple checked that the door was locked tight. He took a last look at Wolf. There was a goose egg on his forehead from where Damon had struck him, and his right hand was bleeding again, though not as badly. His breathing was laboured as well. Even still, he'd refused to unbutton his tight uniform. Wolf must have seen him staring

"Well," he asked. "How do I look?"

"You look like a man who just got his ass handed to him."

Wolf laughed. "I'd like to shee for myshelf."

Damon raised an eyebrow. "You want a mirror?"

Wolf coughed and nodded. Damon, looked to Notty, who shrugged.

"Sure, he'll get you a mirror, but don't think we're your errand boys."

Wolf laughed. "I'd also like a whishkey with lime. Can you get me one, Damon?"

Damon gripped the bars with one hand. "Don't push it. You're a murderer, and don't think we've forgotten."

Damon returned to the hall to find that Brian had asked everyone who wasn't on the mission to leave, aside from Briar who still held a cloth to his cheek. Damon went to take a seat next to Lionel, but Brian stopped him before he could. Rising from his seat at the throne, and waving away his sister's help, he walked over to Damon. His sword lay propped against the arm of the stone throne, but he made no motion to reach for it. When the two were face to face, he looked at Damon as if he were the only other person in the room.

"I counted nine."

Damon didn't have the heart to say anything in return.

Brian continued. "I recall telling you that if anyone got hurt, you'd never be allowed back here.

Damon nodded. He wanted to protest, to say that they had their ship now, but he found the strength to hold his tongue.

Brian put a finger on Damon's chest. "Leave."

Damon did. He didn't fight, or curse, or argue. He simply left.

✳ ✳ ✳

After walking around the island, at least twice over just contemplating what he should do next, it had eventually dawned on him to go back and see Astor. *Surely Brian wouldn't stop me from that.* But the sun was going down, and he would have to wait for tomorrow. He wandering through the trees, collecting dry branches for a fire. It took longer than he would have liked, but before the sky went completely dark, he had started a little fire just outside the treeline on the northeast beachline of the island.

"Still seems pretty cold out, want to come inside?"

Damon furrowed his brow, confused. The voice came from behind him, shallow, and muffled. He turned, and saw a girl standing be the trees. Or what he assumed was a girl. It was hard to tell, because she was wearing a full hazmat suit over her body.

"Dora." He said.

"You know me?" the tone of her voice made it sound like she was smiling. "I'm flattered."

"I'm Damon." he said, getting up. As Dora walked closer, he could see her face flickering in the light of the campfire. She was olive skinned, like someone from Southern Italy or the Greek archipelago. Her hair was brown, and crudely cut to shoulder length. Damon reached out a hand to shake, but hesitated. Dora laughed.

"It's OK," she reached out a gloved hand in response. "As long as I'm in this I can't hurt you."

Damon nodded. "I'll take your word on it."

Dora smiled. "Would you like to come back to my cabin? I don't get too many visitors."

"Sure." Damon smiled back. *It's better than out here.*

They hadn't walked ten minutes before Dora asked the question Damon had hoped to avoid. "So why are you out here alone at night?"

"I went for a walk." Damon answered, hoping it'd be enough. It wasn't.

"Really?" She pondered. "You know there's a whole castle back there. Lots of room to sleep there."

"I know. Just needed a change of scenery."

She chuckled. "Was it Brian? You guys have a fight or something. He can be a little... strong willed, I know."

More than one actually. "No, nothing like that," he lied. *Should I tell her about Gruff?* He wondered. He didn't get the chance, as they passed into a small clearing with a somewhat decrepit looking cabin off to one end.

"Come on," she beckoned.

Dora led Damon into the cabin. It was run down and rotting in places, but somehow still had the air of being humble and homely.

"I can't believe you live here all by yourself," Damon mused.

Dora shrugged, which made a scrunching sound in her hazmat suit. "You get used to it."

"Don't you want to take that off?" Damon asked.

She laughed. "And kill you? No, I'm fine. Sit." She pointed to an old rocking chair by the hearth. "I'll make you some tea."

I hate tea... "Thank you," he said politely.

They talked for the next few hours, until the light of dawn came streaking in through the windows. Dora told Damon all about the island, it's history, and the residents, and probably would have kept talking if Damon hadn't politely excused himself. *I suppose when you live alone, you miss talking with people.* He'd learned all about the generations that had existed on this island. Of how war and strife had brought them down to the measly two dozen here today. How most the residents couldn't even point to the Black Forest on a map, and of how most of them were terrified of one day having the island invaded. Dora told Damon about how really, Lionel's line was usually the one to lead the group at Grimmhaven, but that Brian had taken up the role after Lionel expressed no interest in the role.

Damon had asked her about some of the residents that he didn't know as much about. She told him about how Tyler and Notty never really got along, ironically, and of how Elliot would sometimes come see her and bring her food from the castle's feasts. He also found out that the three Chinese brothers were names Li, Hu, and Bo, and descended from the eldest of what used to be ten identical brothers. Li had eyes that could see miles out, but it didn't do much good as he couldn't quite see the mainland from the island. Hu had the same ability, but with his hearing. Dora explained that all the extra noise once drove him mad, so now he often wore noise-cancelling headphones to stay sane. The last brother, Bo, could blow a powerful wind when he spoke. So more often than not, he'd stay quiet. But Dora had definitely seen him get mad a few times and knock his brothers over with a single word.

Dora led him out, and shut the door behind him. As he began to walk back towards the village, he initially felt relieved, but he found himself also feeling pity. Damon made a mental note to come back when he found the time.

✳✳✳

He passed by the church on the way back. The triplets were in amongst the gravestones, and so was Nikki's friend. The four of them were moving a large stone into the yard. Damon wanted to walk by, but he knew what they were doing, and walked over to pay respects.

"Damon." Nikki's friend said simply.

Damon hadn't known his name, but Dora had mentioned him while talking last night. His name was August, and he was Nikki's cousin in truth. While she got her powers from Jack Frost, August got his from Mother Nature, or so Dora said.

"Hello, August." Damon greeted back. "Do you need a hand?"

August gave Damon a look as though he wasn't sure to trust him. But slowly, he nodded, and allowed Damon to grab a corner. The stone was heavier than it had looked, but between them and the three triplets, the five were able to heave it into place. The stone was flat and blank, but soon, Headstone was at it with a hammer and chisel, and showed why he bore the nickname that he did. When he was done, August knelt in the dirt and pushed in a seed with his thumb. Before Damon's eyes a sprout popped from the ground and bloomed with a single flower. Damon stayed with them for a moment of silence, before moving back on his way to village. His next stop was Nelda's cabin.

"How is he?" Damon asked as soon as Nelda opened the door.

"He's awake, and stable. I did the best I could, but his injury is bad. Remember, I'm no surgeon. Smart thinking with the gold plug in the wound, though. Without it, he would most likely have bled out on the deck. Still, I had to remove it to get the bullet out." She paused. "I'm not going to thank you for what you did. You could have gotten everyone with you killed. You *did* get someone killed. But without that ship, we would have been stranded here. We don't plant enough crops to last us forever."

Damon nodded, and moved past her into the room. Astor was in bed, covers up to his waist. He was shirtless, and a bandage wrapped completely around his midsection. Damon was happy to see it was clean. *No infection, at least as far as I can tell.* Astor smiled when he saw Damon come in. He looked weak, but better than he had.

"How's that sailor," Astor asked.

The question confused Damon. *We're more worried about you, not the sailors.* Then Damon remembered. "You're thinking about Kent?"

"Was that his name? I never got it." Astor frowned. "Is he going to be OK."

Nelda came over, puzzled. "Who's Kent?"

"Astor accidentally touched him in the struggle."

Nelda bit her lip. "Oh. How bad?"

"Right forearm, up to the elbow almost."

She nodded. "Not much I can do about that."

Damon nodded agreement, but Astor didn't want to believe it. "No, you have to do something."

Nelda sat by his bedside. Damon noticed that Astor still had his linen gloves on. Nelda put a hand on his shoulder. "At this point, treating that arm would be like treating a rock. You know better than anyone that your power is irreversible."

Astor nodded glumly.

"He's going to get rich if he sells that arm, though." Damon added, trying to be helpful. Astor didn't smile.

❋ ❋ ❋

"I'll take a look at that Kent guy, if for no other reason than to make Astor feel better." Nelda told Damon as they sat together outside and out of earshot from Astor.

"Agreed", said Damon. "I'll bring him down later today."

"Thanks," said Nelda, kicking a rock down into the brook.

Damon frowned. "Something on your mind?"

She looked away. "You sure I have to stay back?"

Damon nodded. "We need someone back here to take care of the crew while we're away. And Astor for that matter."

"But what if someone gets injured on the trip to the mainland? "What then? You'll need me there."

Damon shook his head. "You're not going into the Black Forest."

"You can't stop me from coming."

"No, I can't." Damon said, sighing. "But Brian can. And as much differences we have, I think he agrees with that."

"Doesn't he still want you gone?"

"He does," Damon admitted. "But Lionel is trying to talk him down. Honestly I think it will come down to whether or not Briar wants me to stay."

"Do you think she will?"

I hope she will. "I don't know," Damon said.

Nelda moved to go back inside. "Well, in the meantime, can you find Tyler for me? I've taken a look at everyone you'd brought on that mission except him. I want to make sure he's OK."

"That's weird, I honestly haven't seen Tyler since the mission. Lionel says he likes to be alone, but I thought someone would have seen him."

"Ya..." said Nelda. "Maybe ask someone."

Oh, I will.

CHAPTER 13

"Wolf!" Damon yelled as he trudged down the stairs into the dungeons. "Wolf, you son of a bitch, what did you do to him?"

Monty caught him on the stairs and pushed him to the wall. "You're not supposed to be here, Grimm."

"Let go of me. I need to talk to the Admiral."

Monty shook his head. "No, I'm taking you to Brian." He made a move to grab Damon by the arm, but instead got an elbow to the side.

Damon pushed past him and into the dungeons below. Three dozen faces stared at him while he made his way to Wolf's cell. His heart skipped a beat when he got to the bars. The cell before him was empty. He hard footsteps trudging up behind him as Monty grabbed him from behind. But no sooner did he do that, did the other boy see it too.

"Where... Where did..." Monty stumbled over his words. "Did you do this?"

Damon scrunched up his face. "No, I didn't. Are you insane?"

"We have to go tell Brian." There was panic in Monty's eyes.

"No, I'll tell Brian. You stay here. Make sure no one else is gone."

Monty nodded subserviently. Apparently, he was much more comfortable taking orders than giving them. Damon left him, and ran as fast as he could up to the mess hall, then up the tower to

Brian's quarters. When he got to the door, he nearly broke the wood pounding so hard. The door flew open.

"What!?" Brian yelled. When he say who was at his door he looked as though he wanted to push Damon back down the stairs.

"I told you to leave."

"Well, I'm still here. But Tyler *is* gone. And so is the Admiral.

Brian's face was awash with concern. "Truly?"

Damon nodded, still out of breath from the climb.

"Show me."

Damon led Brian back to the Dungeon, where Monty reported that everyone else was accounted for, before feebly pleading for forgiveness from Brian.

He ignored the sniveling, and was focussed on the room. "We leave today."

That shocked even Damon. "By we..."

"Yes, you too. Whoever this Admiral is, he didn't sail past this island by accident."

Damon nodded. He was beginning to think the same thing.

"Bring everyone to the hall." Brian turned and went up the stairs. Monty followed, leaving only Damon behind.

It didn't take long to get everyone together. Half of the resident's were already inside Grimmhaven, as everyone was on edge and looking for comfort and security inside the big stone walls. Last inside was Nelda. Once she sat down, Brian began.

"Alright, I need everyone's attention." The room became quiet. "I know that all of you are anxious to know what I plan to do next. Well, I'm going to tell you that you may like the answer and you may not. He paused, gathering himself. "We *are* going to the Black Forest."

Damon looked around the room. There were a few heads nodding, and a few looking obviously stressed by the declaration. Although most only looked ahead sternly. *Either unsure how to process the news, or not wanting to show anyone how they feel,* Damon thought.

Brian continued. "I won't make anyone go that does not want to. But I will say I need all the help I can get. That's why I've decided to take Damon along." That also got mixed reactions. "It was a Grimm who brought us to this island haven, and a Grimm will help get us home." Damon was happy to see Lionel nodding along to that.

"We leave first thing in the morning." Brian added, perhaps realizing that they we're quite ready to leave just yet. "I think whoever is out there in the Forest may have taken Tyler.'

That certainly stirred up a commotion. Brian tried to settle them down quietly, but when that didn't work, he snapped. "ENOUGH!" Brian yelled, and the room hushed. "I don't know why they took him, or even how. All we know is that he's gone right now, and we need to get him back." Damon nodded his approval along with everyone else. Brian stood, and walked towards the stairs leading down to the castle's lower level.

"We lost one of our own recently, I'm sure you don't need reminding of that, though. He began walking down the stairs. "Follow me, I want to show you all something."

Brian led the group down into the dungeons, past the cells, and then through a long corridor. Damon was more than a little surprised at just how far the paths went, and each time he thought they'd reached the end, there was another corridor, or set of stairs, or doorway. By now he knew that they must have been far from the original footprint of Grimmhaven. When Damon paused to get his bearings, he was surprise to see than most, if not all of the others were equally as lost. It seemed that only Brian and Briar knew their way around.

Brian motioned for Damon to continue following him. He did, and the group eventually reached an atrium deep within the bowels of the castle. Brian removed a rose-shaped pendant from his neck and felt the weight in his hand. When he pressed it to the stone wall before him, it creaked, and part of the stone opened to reveal the chamber behind. Damon's eyes widened. Before him was a massive hall, filled with intricately carved stone statues of men and women from folktales, myths, and legends. At each one's feet lay a large wooden chest.

Marlin was the first to see his ancestor, with Merlin the Magician standing tall and proud wrought in stone. Moving past Damon and Brian, the boy shifted his glasses and knelt at the chest. Opening it, he gasping slightly as he pulled out a long indigo robe covered in a pattern of moons and stars. After that came a matching hat, sewn with a wide brim. A staff sat propped up, resting against the Merlin statue's leg. When Marlin reached out and grasped it, blue sparks jumped from the wood. He looked to Brian, too gobsmacked to speak. Brian looked back at him, stone-faced as the statues around them.

Charlotte had already passed them, crawling across the ceiling to where a statue of Arachne stood tall a little way down the hall. She sent a strand of web down into her chest and fished something out of it, crawling back, she leapt down from the ceiling the show the group. In her arms she carried a black steel breastplate with four holes in the back that perfectly matched her arachnid arms. It latched in the front, and she slid it easily over her chest, fitting as though it were made for her.

She glanced over to Brian as she admired the piece. "Why didn't our parents know to take these? If they were going into the Black Forest, they would have come in handy." Damon didn't know whether she was confused or concerned. *Perhaps a bit of both.*

Marlin had donned the cape and was walking over with the staff in hand. "I agree, Brian. How come they didn't come here before they left?"

"Because," said Brian with a sigh. "They didn't know about this room." Everyone in the group seemed to look up at that, even Lionel seemed a little surprised.

"Didn't know?" said Ike. "How could they not have known? How could *we* not have known?" Damon could see his eyes were still red from crying over his lost wings.

Brian looked pained to speak. "Only Briar and I knew; and our mother and father before us, and so on. We were told to keep this vault a secret until any of these items are truly needed. They're priceless. And dangerous, if they were to fall into the wrong hands."

Damon thought for a moment "You must have showed this room to Gruff before we left. He had his father's warhammer, and that armour."

Brian looked pained at the mention of that name. "No, that was taken out of this vault decades ago by one of his ancestors. But originally, yes. It came from here. And where is it now? Unsalvageable, rusting beneath the water. Gone forever, probably."

It was Damon's turn to look pained, but he swallowed his emotions. He was going to apologize again to Brian, but Lionel interrupted his thoughts.

"So why show us now?" asked Lionel. "Our parents could have used this vault; and so could the other half dozen generations who went to the Black Forest before them. What makes us so special?"

"Because we're the last, Lionel, don't you get it?" Brian sounded tired. "What if we go do this, and we don't come back either? That's it for our kind; unless there's some other pocket of folktales that I don't know about?" He looked around as though someone was supposed to answer him. "No? Then it's just us."

Lionel looked at Brian for a long moment. "I understand."

One by one, each of the folktales entered the hall, fanning out to find the stony depiction of their famous ancestor. Some were close to the entrance, and others seemed half a mile away. Damon was familiar with some of the characters etched in stone, but others he was not sure in the slightest who they were supposed to be. Sometimes it was because he truly did not know the story they came from. Other statues had since crumbled away, leaving Damon to puzzle at the features. Each had a pedestal with a name, but most were written in old Germanic, and the others in Greek, so Damon couldn't read them.

Ike had almost run to his predecessor's statue. It was obvious which it was: the one with the wings. He threw open the lid of the chest and screamed out in joy as he pulled a wing pack from the box. Slipping it on over his shoulders, he flapped his arms, and took off into the air, whooping with joy. Damon smiled up at him. The ceiling was high in the vault chamber, but still finite. He pondered whether to call to Ike and tell him to land, but decided against it. *Best not ruin the moment.*

It felt like Christmas walking around the vault and seeing the residents reveal what had been left to them. Monty found he'd been left with a silver flute. Zack had found himself with a candlestick, confusing both of them. And for Notty, there was an old bronze broach in the shape of a crown and star designating the rank of sheriff, as well as a 17th century musket covered in so much dust that Damon nearly mistook it for a stick. Notty had also gone into Tyler Hood's chest which was beneath the statue adjacent to his own.

"For when we find him," he explained, pulling a carved yew bow and quiver from inside. Damon nodded his approval.

He found Brian stopped in front of a statue of a beautiful woman. The stone around her body was carved into the shape of brambles with little stone roses.

"This is Briar Rose," Brian said. "The original," he clarified. "My sister was named for her. So was I, kind of."

Damon walked up next to him. When he looked down, he noticed that the chest at the foot of the statue had already been opened a long time ago. "Your chest is empty."

Brian tapped a finger to his sword hilt. "Christmas came early for Briar and I. We got our gifts a long time ago. Although Briar's dress didn't fit her until recently. For me, I've been practicing with this sword since I was a kid. He unsheathed it. It's the same one my great-great grandfather used to cut away the rose brambles to rescue my great-great grandmother.

"Impressive." Damon mused. "I must have never read the story."

Brian sheathed his sword and looked to Damon, puzzled. "Haven't you opened your chest yet?"

That took Damon aback. "My chest?" He hadn't really considered the possibility that he had a chest down here."

"Of course." Brian walked off and motioned for Damon to follow. He did, and the two walked to the very end of the vault. When they got there, Damon looked up to see the statue of a man standing with a writing quill and parchment.

"I don't know who that is."

"Sure you do," said Brian.

Damon nodded. *It had to be Jacob Grimm.* Kneeling, he lifted the lid of the old chest, the hinges creaking with age as he did. Frowning, he saw nothing inside, so he felt around the bottom until he found it. Lifting it up, he held it to the light of the torch on the wall.

"It's a pen," Damon said, sorely lacking in his attempt to mask his disappointment. It was a quill technically, he knew. But big difference that made. He looked over to Brian and gestured to his scabbard. "Bit of a step down from that."

Brian shrugged. "Well, the pen is... well, you know the rest."

✳ ✳ ✳

That evening it was decided. The Blacktooth was to set sail for the mainland just after the sun had risen. The crew had done a good job repairing her after Marlin's lightning, but some work still had to be done. Luckily, the fire hadn't burned through the metal hull, and the ship could sail without taking water. Damon had been designated as helmsman, being the only actual member of the navy amongst them. Brian had obviously been earmarked as Captain, with Notty as his first mate. With them were coming Lionel, Theodore,

Nikki, Charlotte, Monty, Woody, Ike, Marlin, Zack, August, Elliot, and all three of the triplets; Li, Hu, and Bo. Also: Briar, if she had her way that was. Brian was adamant to stop her from coming, but the way Damon saw it, she was getting onboard one way or another.

Nelda and Headstone were staying behind to care for the Blacktooth's crew, as well as for Astor as he recovered. He was still too weak to walk, but his powers still worked, and they had made sure to get lots of gold from him before leaving. Brian said that having a little extra could come in handy down the line. Astor was sad to have to stay behind, but happy to help in the little way that he could from his bed. Dora had also stayed behind against her will. Brian had gone by last night to let her know what was happening. She insisted on being there to help. But Brian had flat out denied her on the spot. She was too dangerous to have around; however good her intentions were. One break in the hazmat suit she wore, and they would all be in serious trouble.

As the light of the dawn cracked the sky from over the water, Damon was already awake and ready to go. He hadn't slept at all last night in truth, but that came as no surprise. He was worried. He knew that where they were going and what they were doing was dangerous. And in the short time he'd come to know everyone here, he'd come to grow a bond with them. *A week ago, if someone had told me fairy tales were real, I would have laughed in their face. Now, I call them my friends.* He stretched, and began walking the beach over to the ship. Damon no longer wore his uniform, instead electing to go with clothes Lionel had lent to him. They were too big for him, but he felt much more comfortable in them, both physically and symbolically.

His mind was focused mostly on Admiral Wolf and how he had escaped the dungeon. No matter how many times he ran it through his head he couldn't parse it out. His only solution was that someone must have let him out. But he had no answer as to who. There was no motive, and not much of an opportunity. Besides, if Wolf got out that way, Damon had no illusions that he'd be first on his target list.

That, or he would have set the rest of the crew free. *It just doesn't make sense.* The same thoughts went through his head about Tyler. That disappearance had also stumped him.

Climbing the ramp to the deck of the ship, Damon greeted Notty, who was staring off over the prow while cleaning his new musket.

"You know, there were plenty of modern rifles aboard when we took the ship. You're welcome to one of those."

Notty shook his head. Damon noticed the sun glinting off the sheriff's broach pinning Notty's red capelet to his shirt. "I'll stick with this one, thanks."

Damon shrugged. "Suit yourself." *But if I need you to save my ass, you better have something better than that boomstick to do it.*

Brian was also already onboard in the control room. Briar stood nest to him; her hair pinned up in a braid over one shoulder. She gave Damon a coy smile and a little wave. Damon didn't smile back. *Not this time, that got me in enough trouble already.*

"Ready?" asked Damon to Brian. He saw Briar's smile fade from the corner of his eye.

"As soon as everyone is on board. Are you sure you can sail this thing?"

Damon bit his lip. "If I can't, there's the original helmsman in Grimmhaven. If nothing else, we bring him here to do it."

Brian nodded, satisfied. "And you can get us into town?"

"I'll do my best. Like I said, my parent's old abandoned house is there. There's more than enough room to stay for a few days while we set out our plan."

"And enough room for our parents as well when we find them?"

Damon gave him a half-smile. "Not really, but we'll make it work, won't we?"

Brian smiled back. The swelling around his right eye had gone down to the point where he could open it once again. Still, that half of his face was bruised purple and yellow and Damon still felt bad about it. Instinctively, he touched his own cheek. The cut had been deep, and ran horizontal under his left eye for at least two inches across. The scab was still healing, and Damon had no doubt that he'd be left with a scar when it was done.

Out on deck, Damon watched Ike flying overhead. He couldn't help but smile at how happy he had become since reclaiming his wings. Beside him, Lionel was climbing up the ramp. Damon hardly recognized him. The young man had shaved the fur on his face to a tidy trim, and cut his hair short. Over his chest, he wore a breastplate of blue enameled steel that he'd gotten from the vault, and he'd donned his clean clothes where he usually wore dusty tan shorts.

"You're all gussied up."

Lionel grinned. "This could be it. Figured if something happens, I should look the part of a hero. Besides, if we... *when* we find our parents, I want my dad to be proud"

Damon placed a hand on his shoulder. 'I'm sure he will be."

As the rest filed on board, Damon left Lionel to take his position at the helm. Nelda waved up at them from the shoreline as the Blacktooth pulled back into the water.

Here we go.

CHAPTER 14

The Blacktooth landed after what seemed like days at sea. Navigating the North Sea turned out to be much harder than any of them had anticipated. More than once, they had had to send Ike high into the sky to tell them if they were heading the right way. Damon was embarrassed to admit just how close he came to landing them in Sweden. *Docking* was also a stretch. In truth, they had done little more than *stop* the boat on a random beach on the north shore of Germany. Damon figured the locals wouldn't take too kindly to a boat full of freaks showing up in their harbour. Charlotte and Lionel especially would have some explaining to do. Instead, they elected to sail for a beach far enough away from any big cities that they may have a chance at not running across anyone at all. Although Damon still didn't want to risk it. As they had come within sight of the shore, he had Marlin shroud the ship in a thick fog. A big grey cloud on the water would be confusing to any onlooker, but it was at least better than a Military vessel from the UK.

Damon was shocked at just how thick the fog Marlin was able to conjure; and with such ease. Ever since he'd obtained his ancestor's staff, he'd scarcely put it down. Damon wouldn't have been surprised if he'd learned that the boy slept with it. But it *had* channeled Marlin's power's immensely, and that eased Damon's heart.

In the short few weeks that he'd known the small group of outcast fables, he'd become more attached to them than he had with anyone else in his life beforehand. Maybe it was because he was, in a way, one of them. *Maybe*. Regardless, Damon knew that whatever they were sailing towards, it was going to be dangerous. *Very* dangerous. Damon still wasn't over the loss of Gruff. And Damon didn't even *like* Gruff.

He wondered if that's what Brian was thinking about too. The boy was standing at the helm of the ship, looking ponderously into the thick fog around the ship, as if trying to see something in the grey swirls. One hand was as ever on the hilt of his sword. Perhaps he was thinking of his sister; Briar had chosen to come with them, despite all Brian's protesting. He had wanted her to stay back and watch over the actual crew of the Blacktooth with Nelda until they returned. *If we return*. Damon thought bitterly.

Damon was also thinking about Astor. Back in the Hall of Fables, they had found King Midas' cloth-of-gold gloves and golden crown, but Brian had decided to take neither of them. The crown Damon understood. Half the people in that castle were descended from this king or that one, and it would have been wretchedly pompous to go around Grimmhaven wearing a crown. But the gloves? Damon shrugged it off. Not important enough to ask. Besides, he had other things on his mind. Astor had been in an out of conscious just before they'd shipped off. Luckily, he was awake when Damon had gone to see him.

"You know, I've never even been to the mainland before," Astor had said.

Damon was surprised by that. "Really? You pass as normal as long as you don't touch anything. Besides, it's *your* gold that pays for everything."

Astor smiled at that. "Does it really surprise you that *I* never left the island?"

"It surprises me more that you're sad that you're not leaving the island now. You know what's in the Black Forest."

Astor nodded. "My father told me the story of how we were run out of our homes there, but he never went into which were the ones to kick us out."

Damon gently clapped him on the back and smiled warmly. "I'll let you know when we're back."

Marlin tapped the butt of his staff on the deck three times, taking Damon from his thoughts, and causing the fog around them to begin to fizzle like smoke after fireworks. He smiled at Damon for his work, and Damon smiled back. They were alone on the beach for now, but there was no telling if it'd be that way for long. Brian lowered the ramp, and as quickly as they could, the group convened on the sand below. Ike was the last down, after he'd done an aerial sweep.

"No one," he informed Damon, and pointing he said. "That way there's a forest about a mile south. We can go through it, and follow the creek most of the way to the Black Forest."

Damon shook his head. "Too long, and too many towns and cities in the way. You want to be on News at 11:00? We'll have to be more subtle."

He turned to Brian. "Where do you normally buy your supplies?"

Brian pointed down the road a ways. "A town, about a mile that way. Why?"

Damon grinned. "I have an idea."

✳ ✳ ✳

The town Brian was referring to was Wremen. The shop: a local place called Seemannsschatz, or *Sailor's Bounty*. The man behind the counter was an older fellow, with grey hair drooping down to his shoulders, and a handlebar moustache that drooped past his chin and reminded Damon of Lemmy Kilmister. On his left hand, he was missing the last joint of his middle finger. Damon approached him, ready to see how much of his German he remembered. Brian spoke first, though, and Damon was surprised (and a bit relieved) to learn that the man spoke fluent English.

"Brian!" He smiled. "I haven't seen you in a while, boy! How have you been?" He turned his gaze to Damon. "And who's your friend?"

"It's been a while, Frank. This is Damon, an... acquaintance of mine."

Frank sucked in through his teeth. "I hope he didn't give you that shiner there." Brian laughed. From his bag, he heaved a large piece of driftwood that Astor had turned gold for them. It clunked loudly as it hit the counter. At the same time, Frank's jaw nearly hit the floor.

"I suppose... that you'll be needing something hard to get."

"We need a bus." It was Damon who said it.

Frank looked at him with glazed eyes and a raised eyebrow. "I don't *have* a bus, and I don't know who *you* are." He muttered something under his breath in German. Damon knew exactly what he said, but chose to ignore it and pretend that he didn't understand.

"That's twenty-five pounds of gold in front of you. I think you can get us a bus."

Frank leaned over the counter. "I don't know if you know how this transaction works, boy, so I'll explain it. Brian brings me golden... things. I don't ask how he gets them; I don't ask where he gets them. In return, I give him supplies from my storeroom. Or, he tells me what he needs, and the next time he comes, I have it in the storeroom for him." He motioned to the golden driftwood. "See this?" I can't spend *this*. I'll have to have it smelted into bars, then I exchange those bars for money, and *then* I can buy the stuff. Do you expect me to show up to the dealership with a hunk of gold and for them to take me seriously?"

Damon didn't answer. He didn't have one. But Brian was letting him ramble. When it was clear Frank was done, Brian placed a hand on the counter and said. "The gold isn't for you to buy a bus. It's for your bus. Your band's tour bus."

That made Damon raise an eyebrow. "You have a tour bus?"

Frank hymned and hawed. "It's more of a tour... van. I may have exaggerated. But she ain't for sale, Brian."

Brian looked Frank in the eye, and without flinching, placed a *second* golden driftwood on the table. It too clunked loudly. Frank bit his lip.

"That's fifty pounds of gold for one van. Come on Frank, you know you want it."

Frank closed his eyes and shook his head. "Screw you Brian, I loved that van." He turned and pulled a key from the wall and tossed it to him. "Treat her right, you hear? She's out back near the shed. May need a fill-up if you intend on taking her far...Where *are* you taking her?"

Damon laughed as the two of them left out the shop's back door. "The forest." He walked away and laughed at the horrified expression on Frank's face as the door shut behind them.

Out back, Damon sat in the driver's seat, and turned the key in the ignition. The van roared to life. Brian was sitting in the passenger seat and jumped near off his seat. *I don't think he's ever been in a car.* Damon saw how stressed Brian looked and look pity on him, trying to drum up some small-talk as they pulled out onto the road back towards the beach where they had left the others.

"Frank seems nice."

Brian nodded, as he gripped the door furiously with one hand. *This is going to be an interesting trip.*

✸✸✸

The passenger van was luckily able to fit everyone, but barely. It was going to be a long drive. Brian had thrown up no less than three times on their way back to the beach, and Damon expected that he wasn't done yet. Right now, Brian was off in the bushes, with Woody rubbing his back as he heaved whatever was left in his stomach into the weeds.

Notty came up beside Damon. "You'd think he'd be fine with a car since he's fine on a boat."

Damon chuckled. "Maybe they're two different things." He looked over at Notty. "How would you know; you've never driven either."

Notty smiled. "I've made a few supply runs for the group. Unlike Brian, I don't like walking back each time."

Damon laughed again. "I can't imagine you have a license." Notty only smiled. "Oh!" Damon exclaimed as he remembered. "This is yours." He handed the revolver back to Notty, who took it graciously.

"Thanks, I hope it came in handy."

Damon gave him a sympathetic look. "They've come a little way since that old relic. I hope you aren't offended that it didn't get much use."

"Only a little," Notty said. "By the way, how's the cheek?"

They grinned at each other as Brian walked up to them, wiping his mouth.

"Ready to go?" asked Damon.

"No," said Brian. "But let's go."

It was a long trip across Germany with eighteen people cramped into one passenger van. Well, seventeen really since Theodore could sit on the dashboard. Still, Zack and the triplets had to cram in where the luggage would normally go in the back. It was also lucky that there were blinds on some of the back windows. That was where Lionel, Charlotte, and Elliot sat. Elliot had the hardest time, since when he sat up straight, his horns bumped the roof of the vehicle. But even with all that, they made it to Hornberg without so much as an incident, and only two stops for gas and such.

Damon couldn't help but feel an overwhelming sense of nostalgia as he pasted the small rusty road sign leading them into town. It was late, at least 1:00 am, and pitch black out. It was perfect for sneaking everyone into his old abandoned house. Damon turned the van down a dirt road and checked the fuel gauge. The needle quavered just above E. *Good timing.*

Most of the group was sleeping as he pulled into the lot behind the house. Brian wasn't, though, awake and alert as ever. He had at least gotten over his motion sickness, though. *Or swallowed it, so to speak,* Damon thought.

"Is this the place?" Brian asked.

Damon nodded. "This is the place."

Brian unbuckled his seatbelt and began to open the door.

"Hang on," Damon cautioned. "Let me see if the coast is clear."

Brian raised an eyebrow. "Why can't I do that?"

"You're wearing a sword."

Brian glanced down. "Right." He sat back in his seat. Briar yawned and stretched from the seat behind him.

"Are we here?"

"Yes," Damon said. "Wake the others, too."

Briar rubbed her eye with the palm of her hand. "You do it," said muttered, and lulled off again.

Brian rolled his eyes, and moved back to start waking the group while Damon left the van wand walked up to his old home. It was more or less just as he remembered it, with it's dark wood panelling and oak door painted burgundy. The grass had been mowed, but that wasn't a surprise. The hamlet always liked keeping up appearances; and an old abandoned house was no good for that. He checked to make sure none of the neighbors were watching and jiggled the door handle. *Locked.*

He probably had a key somewhere in his London flat, but no way to get that now. Kneeling, he found a heavy pointed rock amongst some hedges by the door. Weighing it in his hand, he gripped it, pointed end down, and beat the doorknob with it. The resulting *BANG* of stone on metal made Damon cringe and look around. No lights had gone on, so he hit it again. *BANG!* The wood was thick, but also old, and after three hits the knob cracked from its place in the door. Damon jigged it, and smiled as the door creaked open. He waved to Brian and went inside.

When he entered the front foyer and looked around, Damon was puzzled to see that it was furnished. There was new rug on the floor, and an end table with family photographs. *Oh no.*

"Break into my house, will you!? The voice was in German, and very angry. Damon whipped his head around just in time to catch a fist against his injured cheek. It was a glancing blow, but enough to knock him back against the wall. His leg knocked the end table, and framed photos shattered on the ground.

It was dark, but Damon's eyes had already adjusted enough to see that the man held a shotgun. Panic set in, and Damon scampered back out the door. Or at least, he tried to. The man was bigger than Damon, and a burly hand caught him by the shirt and wrenched him back inside and onto the floor.

"You aren't going anywhere." He pointed the barrel of his gun at Damon. 'Don't move. Josie! Call the police!"

Damon raised his hands in a show of surrender. *If that goes off, it'll bring the whole town down on us. But if the police are called... its all over.* Luckily, Damon didn't have to think long on what to do. He watched as the barrel of the man's shotgun frosted with ice. He didn't even seem to notice, until his hands started to frost as well. Gasping, he dropped the weapon. Damon wasted no time. Rushing upstairs, he burst into the master bedroom, where a young woman in her nightgown shrieked and dropped the phone she was dialing. A baby cried out from a crib in the corner. *Perfect. Just perfect,* he though.

"It's OK!" Damon tried to reassure her in German. "I'm not going to hurt you!"

Luckily, she didn't scream again, only whimpered. The baby still cried out, though, but Damon didn't know what to do about that. *It's ok*, he told himself. *A crying baby won't draw any attention.* Damon reached down and picked the phone off the floor.

"Please, Miss. Go make sure your baby is OK." Damon tried to sound reassuring.

She looked at him with suspicion, but allowed herself to walk past the stranger and pick up the crying child from where he lay. Damon put the phone in his pocket and made his way downstairs. The lights were on now, and everyone had made their way into the house, with the door shut behind them. *Although not locked, to be sure.* The man of the house was sitting cross-legged in the middle of the front foyer. His arms were webbed tight behind his back, and another web was over his mouth.

He jerked on the floor, attempting to set himself free. He was angry, understandably so, but Damon was surprised to see that he was not scared at the sight of them. Even with Charlotte standing before him, eight limbs and all, he did not flinch. Damon knelt before him, and peeled the webbing from his mouth. The man sputtered a bit as a few bits had found their way into his mouth. He spit them onto the floor before looking back at Damon with glaring blue eyes.

"You're them from the forest, you lot are."

That made Damon's ear's prick up. "No. Do you know them?"

"What's he saying?" asked Theodore. Damon forgot that none of the others spoke German.

"Don't play games." The man continued. "I've seen you. I know what you are."

"So, what are we?"

"Monsters!" He began to struggle again with his bondage.

Damon gave him a sign to calm down. "I'm not a monster. My name is Damon."

He seemed to calm a little at that. "Johann. Johann Werner"

Johann? Damon's jaw nearly dropped. His mind flashed back to his childhood. All the times he'd been bullied. All the stolen change. And especially the incident at the Christmas market. In the dark it had been hard to see, but now in the light he could see the resemblance to his childhood classmate was uncanny. His hair had been buzzed, and his face had sprouted a beard, but it was the same mousy reddish-brown Damon had known.

"Do you remember me?" Damon asked.

Johann shook his head. "Should I?"

That pissed Damon off more than he thought it would. He looked Johann in the eye. "It's me. Damon Grimm. The *freak*."

Understanding lit like a fire in Johann's eyes. "Damon... it is you... you're... you're one of them?"

Damon thought about that for a moment. "Yes. I am."

"What should we do with him?" asked Brian.

Damon pondered for a moment. "Take him to the living room. Leave him webbed for now, but be gentle. Brian nodded, and he and Lionel took Johann by the arms. He went without much of a struggle.

Damon excused himself from the group to go to the washroom. It had been a long trip, and there was only so long he could go. When he was done, he stood at the sink and peered at his face. He hadn't bathed since before leaving London. Unless of course you could count leaping into the sea. *Or being thrown into it*. He bent over, and let the water from the tap wash over his face. Coming up, he rubbed the water over his skin and in his eyes. Looking back in the mirror, Damon nearly had a heart attack.

A girl was standing behind him. He didn't recognize her, but she had the same red hair as Johann so she must have been a relative. Damon turned around, but to his confusion, no one was there. Puzzled he looked back in the mirror. *She's still there, though*. He looked closer, nearly pressing his nose to the mirror. The girl grinned. Suddenly, she reached forward, and her hand shot straight through the mirror, as if it wasn't there, catching Damon by the throat. He struggled, but was off balance. He fought back, but the girl pulled harder, and Damon went head over heels over top of the sink, and in through the mirror.

CHAPTER 15

Damon scrambled to his feet, standing in the dirt. He was no longer inside of his parent's old house. Instead, he was in the middle of the Black Forest. He looked around, beginning to panic. The girl was there. She was standing in front of him. She was real now, no longer a ghost in a mirror. Behind him *was* a mirror though, hanging off a nearby tree. For some reason, Damon tried to scamper back through, but only wound up bumping his hands on it. The girl sniggered.

Damon turned. "Who are you." He started moving forward but someone grabbed him from behind. At first Damon thought it was a bear, but in reality, it was a man wearing a bear pelt. Although, he was as big as a small bear, and smelled like a wild animal. His nails were long and unkept, and they dug into Damon's wrist where he gripped him.

Another man leapt down from a tree. He had the feet and tail of a monkey and grinned giddily at Damon. Another few shapes began emerging from the shadows, but before Damon could make them out. The monkey-man leapt forward, nearly dancing at him, and struck Damon across the head with a staff. Everything went back.

Damon awoke to find himself in a small wooden lean-to with his hands shackled to the wall. He pulled on the chain, but it was stuck tight. Grunting, he tried to slip his one hand from the fetter, but to no luck.

"Finally." A voice said from across the room.

Damon squinted. Admiral Wolf sat with his legs up on a table smoking a pipe and looking generally pleased with himself.

"I shuppose that the tablesh have turned... He chewed his tongue. "Shcrew it, I'm taking theesh thingsh out now." Damon watched as with a gloved hand, Wolf ripped what looked like dentures from off his teeth and threw them to the ground, revealing two rows of sharp canines beneath. "There," he said, without a hint of a lisp. "That's better." He smiled a toothy grin at Damon.

Damon looked upon him with a mix of horror and fascination. "So, who are you, really?"

Wolf smiled, and took a black leather glove off his hard, revealing a grey furry hand with long gnarled yellow fingernails. "You'll figure it out."

"Guess I wasn't the only one using a false name."

Wolf smirked. "My, what a big brain you have."

Damon's eyes fixated on a cloak in the corner. He knew who's it was. "What did you do with Tyler?"

"Is that his name?" Wolf laughed, knocking the ashes from his pipe into an ashtray. "Before you ask, he's fine. Just a little roughed up." He took a long drag. "Can you believe it? Sara thought that he was you! You don't even look alike!"

Damon didn't understand. "Why me?"

"Do you really have to ask that, *Mr. Grimm*?"

Damon tried to rise to his feet, but the chains weren't long enough, and he slumped back down. His temples were pounding. "You knew who I was from the moment you saw me. How is that possible? I wasn't even set to depart with you on the Blacktooth. I was practically a stowaway." Damon was so confused... questions swam in his head like fish eating at his brain.

Wolf shrugged. "You *were* going to set out with me... but on my next trip out. The way I see it, you just moved the plan up about six months. I've been watching your story play out since you came to my attention after beating the snot out of poor old Grendelson. He was one of mine, you know."

Wolf looked as though he wanted to say something else. Damon wasn't sure *what* to say, so after a few moments of awkward silence, Wolf continued.

"I fucked up, you know." He took another puff. "I assumed the Dutchman boy was one of ours. Boy, was I wrong! After I found that out, I assumed you were dead, but I had to sail back just to make sure. Lucky for me, you were still kicking. And here you are now." He laughed. "Not that you made it easy for me, though." He pulled up his shirt for Damon to see. Wolf's chest was covered in thick hair, but beneath that it was a deep purple down both sides of his body. He lowered the shirt, and held up his right paw. There was a gnarly scab dead centre of the palm.

Damon frowned. "So, what now? You break my ribs in return?"

Wolf laughed again, a little too hard. He winced and grabbed his side. "No; Bossman needs you." He got up from his chair. "Come on." Wolf unhooked Damon's first hand from the wall.

Naturally, Damon took a swing at him as he unlocked the second one. A jab, right for the ribs. Wolf saw it coming a mile away. He pinned Damon to the wall with a paw and snarled at him, getting right up in Damon's face. "Just because the boss says I'm not supposed to rough you up, doesn't mean I won't."

"Who is this boss, anyway?"

"You think I'm telling you anything?"

"I see no reason not to."

"I do." He shoved Damon so he stumbled forward. "Walk."

Damon opened the door of the lean to.

"MOVE!"

Damon leapt back out of surprise and confusion. It was a good thing he did, as a bolt of lightning came arcing through the door. It struck the back wall of the lean to, setting it alight, and causing Wolf to cry out in a rage. Damon wasted no time. Hoping that was

Marlin, he booked it through the open doorway into the night. He had no idea where to go, but Lionel grabbed him by the shoulders. "This way."

Wolf was already at the door, about to give chase when Elliot grappled him. The lanky boy was thin, but strong, and he and Wolf shoved at each other, until Elliot's hoof slipped in the mud, and Wolf pushed him to the ground. Damon was already off and running with Lionel bounding on all fours at his side. "How did you find me?"

"As soon as we'd realized you disappeared, we all started looking. Ike was flying over the forest and saw them taking you into the hut. I guess its luck you were still inside. He smiled. "Good thing we had Zack with us."

When they came into a nearby clearing, Damon was happy to see the others all there; including Tyler who was sitting on a log next to Briar. He smiled at Damon as they got near.

"Sorry," he said. His face was slightly bruised, but nothing major or life threatening.

Damon looked at him and frowned. "For what?"

"They told me about Gruff. If I was there... I could have done something. I should have been there." He looked down at the ground. His head was covered in a cowl, but Damon saw a tear drip down from beneath it and land in the dirt. He was doing to console him, but was interrupted when Ike landed behind him.

"They know were here. They're coming."

'Who?" said Brian. "How many?"

"Ten? Maybe? I don't know who they are. Except the Wolf guy."

Elliot came trotting up through the bushes. Hot on his tail was Wolf, nearly running on all fours. Elliot stopped in the middle of the group; Wolf, at the edge of the clearing.

"There's no more running, Grimm," he called out.

From all around them, others started appearing out of the darkness. Damon turned to see the monkey-man hop down from a nearby tree. There were two men that appeared behind the group. One was no older than Damon, and wore loose clothes. He was handsome, and his hair was pulled down across one eye. The other was older, and had a scar across one cheek. There was a mirror hanging off one of the trees, and through it stepped the girl that had taken Damon here. The man in the bearskin cloak came from the east, and August nearly leapt out of his skin when he saw him.

Damon was getting nervous. "We can't stay here." He whispered to Brian."

"Agreed. We need to choose the best way out."

Damon glanced around. "There's no one in our way if we all run to the west."

Brian nodded. "You lead everyone back into town, I'll hold them off." He unsheathed his sword from its scabbard. That made Wolf laugh.

"Trying to be a hero, eh?"

Brian didn't take his eyes off the Admiral. "Go, now." He told Damon.

"Alright I'll-" but no sooner than he had started speaking was there a new man standing in the direction in which Damon had intended to flee. And this one was very familiar. He stood seven feet tall, or near enough, and was covered in matte black fur with two white curled horns protruding from his brow. The man smiled the same smile Damon remembered from so long ago

Its him. It's the creature. He froze in awe and terror, his childhood nightmare standing before him after all these years.

"DAMON, MOVE!" Lionel shoved him to the ground just as a boulder came hurtling past his head. A huge lumbering figure came forward from the trees, and another rock thumped the ground next to them, sending tremors across the dirt.

"He needs the one on the ground alive!" called out Wolf to his cohorts. "The rest are fair game!"

Brian gave a cry and charged headlong at Wolf, Notty, Monty, and Woody all running close behind. The Admiral roared and met them head-on. Ike took to the sky, and Charlotte began spinning a protective web. Zack brought Tyler the yew bow and quiver that they had gotten in the Hall of Fables. Tyler thanked him, and nocked an arrow to the string, but it was obvious that not all his strength was with him. Lionel was helping Damon to his feet.

"Are you OK?" The voice was Briar's. She had rushed over and was knelt beside him.

"I'm fine," he said. But even as the words came out of his mouth, another stone was dropping down from the sky. Damon gasped Briar's shoulders and pulled her down beside him. Vines began to grow around them like a brown lattice, and stopped the momentum of the falling boulder, cracking beneath its weight. Damon looked over to see August focussing intently. Damon smiled to him as a gesture of thanks. August smiled back, but the smile faded as the man in the bearskin cloak came up behind him, and lifted August off the ground in a bear-hug.

Damon meant to help him, but his attention was shifted once again as a loud BANG was heard through the field. Notty had fired his musket nearly point-blank at Wolf. The shot had only grazed the Admiral's arm, though, and served no more purpose than to make him angry. Damon watched as he swung a meaty paw at Notty, raking him across the neck and chest with his yellow claws. As Notty fell to the ground, Brian was already moving in with his sword.

Across the field, Marlin was in in his own predicament. A man with a face painted to look like a skull was trying to wrestle his staff from him. The staff sizzled with red sparks and his attacker let go. Marlin swung, and knocked him with the butt end. Zack was cowering in behind. Brave as the eight-year-old was, he far too young for this. *As if the rest of us aren't also too young.* Damon thought grimly.

Damon knew that he had to do something. But everything around him was happening so fast, it was impossible to keep track of it all. He watched as one of the triplets got thrown into the bushes by the man with a scar. Another of them was already there, face down, and the third was nowhere to be seen. The girl from the mirror, the one Wolf had called Sara, had a knife and was wielding it at Nikki. Damon also saw what looked to be a metal man with a woodcutter's axe trying to catch Charlotte, who was leaping from tree to tree. But it was Briar who seemed to be in the most trouble. She had run off, and now she faced down the black horned beast before her.

Damon ran to her, with Lionel sprinting off in a different direction to help another of the Grimmhaven residents. Damon snatched a dead branch from off the ground as he went as the best weapon he could muster. He ran as fast as his feet could take him, but his path was blocked by a hooded man who stepped up to Damon. In the dark, it was impossible to see the features of the man's face. He reached a hand out to grab Damon, so Damon swung the stick as hard as he could. It knocked his head sideways with a *SNAP*. When the man looked back at Damon, he had a gash across the entire length of his face. *But no blood.* As he made another grab at Damon, the hood fell back from his head, revealing the face underneath was not flash and bone, but plastic. *A mannequin head?* He used his stick to bump it in the forehead. A buckle snapped, and the head rolled off his shoulders; bouncing into the grass. But this didn't phase Damon's opponent. He made a third grab for Damon, and this time he caught him by the collar.

"Get off!" Damon kicked forward and knocked the headless man to the ground before him. Scrambling, he ran past to help Briar. But Brian had gotten there first. He had disengaged with the fight with Wolf to help his sister, but now he too was in trouble. The black horned beast had each of them at bay. Brian's sword lay yards away, and his armour was dinted half a dozen times. Damon could hear Wolf barking orders in the middle of the fray.

"Domerick! Help Alejandro!"

The handsome boy rushed from where he was heading off Elliot to go flank Marlin, who seemed to be getting the upper-hand on his morbid adversary.

"Davey, stop fucking around and be useful." The scarred man moved in on Tyler, who was still struggling with his bow.

"Klaus!" Wolf called out, and the black beast looked up. "Forget the flower bitch. Grab the boy!" The beast known as Klaus nodded, and knocked Briar to the dirt with the back of his hand. Brian immediately dropped to her side.

Damon grabbed his sword from the dirt. Brian hardly even noticed. "Sorry, I need this," Damon said anyways. He had never held a sword before, and the weight was awkward in his hands. The monster towered over him. "I saw you as a child," he called up. "I wasn't sure you were even real."

Klaus was disinterested. Lowering, his head, he meant to butt Damon with his horns, but lighting flashed and lit the area, blinding Damon, and leaving Klaus reeling, the fur singed on his chest. Damon saw Marlin with his staff pointed in his direction. There was no time to rest, though.

"Fog!" he called. "Marlin, do it!"

Marlin nodded, and a thick mist began bellowing around him. As it expanded out, it covered Brian and Briar, hiding them from view. But before it could fully condense, Damon saw the man with the painted face named Alejandro as he grabbed Marlin from behind. His touch was like Astor's. But instead of gold, what this man touched turned black as death. Marlin screamed, as the rot spread up from his neck and shoulders, and down past his chest. Marlin collapsed to his knees, then his stomach, as his glasses fell off his face and shattered on the ground.

Nikki panicked from where she stood watching in the clearing. Horrified, she called out Marlin's name, but no answer came. A stream of frosted air emanated from her hand, condensing the air coming towards Alejandro. Domerick smirked. The handsome boy stood behind Alejandro. Snapping his fingers, the frozen air melted into rain in front of them, the icy air never reaching its target. Domerick sniggered. Moving forward he held his hand up high.

"My turn."

The trees closest to the group burst suddenly into flames. Damon moved forward, but Domerick only smirked and shot a hand out on front of him. Damon felt a blast of hot air, as if from a furnace. The heat sent him reeling to the side, his cheek and hand singed.

Screaming came from behind him. Domerick had made all the surrounding wood in the clearing catch fire. All of it. And that included Woody. Damon watched in horror as his skin turned black and smouldered. Monty was laying on the ground next to him. Damon wasn't sure if the fight with Wolf had left him unconscious or dead. Either way, he could be no help to his burning friend.

"Bastard!" Damon called.

Domerick shrugged. "Wolf said he's expendable."

Smoke began to fill the clearing. The fire began spreading outwards, catching more and more trees. "Nikki! You need to stop this!"

But Nikki was in her own trouble. The giant who had been throwing rocks at Damon now had her in a big meaty hand. Damon started to panic. *This is what happened to their parents. This is why they never came back.*

Brian let out a vicious scream and came barrelling up past Damon, swiping the sword from his hand as he did. The steel glinted in the light of the fire as he swung it towards Domerick. The steel caught flesh, and cut deep into his chest. Wide eyed, he fell backwards, clutching at the red stain swelling on his shirt. Brian cocked back for a second swing, but couldn't deliver it before wolf had him pinned.

Fire burned all around them. More than half of Damon's group was lying on the ground. Worse, he had no idea if they needed help, or if they're gone already. Brian struggled in Wolf's arms, kicking his legs and trying to free himself.

Damon knew that there was only one thing he could do. "You only want, me, right? OK then. Come get me."

He took off running, not looking back, not knowing where he was going. He scanned for a route of escape, but the wall of fire had grown too high, and he was trapped. There was only one way out that he could think of going. He turned, and saw that the Black Forest inhabitants had him cornered. He reached out and grabbed Sara, pulling her to his chest. Damon took the knife from her, and turned it on her throat. She gasped lightly. She was only twelve or thirteen. Damon felt horrible, but he had to do it. He dragged her backwards, threatening the whole time with the knife, to the tree that had the mirror.

"Take me through," he demanded.

"No," she refused as she kicked him in the shin. Damon ignored the pain and pressed the knife harder. Her eyes filled with fear, and Damon watched the mirror shimmer. He stepped in when Alejandro, the man with a face painted like a skull, grabbed him on the shoulder. He felt searing pain shoot down his arm and down his side. Letting himself fall, he watched as the burning forest slipped away, and suddenly he was tumbling down a hill in some other place entirely.

CHAPTER 16

Damon lay splayed out on the ground at the bottom of a rocky ridge. Everything ached. Far off in the distance he could see smoke billowing out over the trees. He could also hear the sound of a firetruck wailing down a nearby roadway. That made him chuckle. It was somehow... a small bit of *normal* in the world of wonders he'd found himself in.

He hoped more than anything that Wolf's posse had dispersed to look for him. If not, all of the people he'd come to know were as good as dead. *Lionel, and Theodore, and Nikki, and Brian, and Briar. We should have never come; never have tried to be heroes.* He tried to sit up, but the pain in his side was immense. Grimacing, he touched the flesh through his shirt and was concerned to find that it was spongey. After that, he was too afraid to actually *lift* his shirt and look.

Beside him, laying face down, was Sara. Her red hair straw-like hair sprawled out like a crimson web. She was breathing, but must have hit her head on the way down. She was out cold. *Good. Without her, they can't follow me.* Damon was still lost, though. At least in part. He knew where the battle had taken place by the smoke, but he had no intention of going back there. He had to find his way back to town. As far as that went, Damon didn't know where it was. He decided to go in the direction the siren sound had come from. At least that meant a road. He considered carrying Sara back with him, but on the first step he took, a pain shot through him and he quickly decided against it. *Lost in the Black Forest again*, he thought.

It was still relatively dark out, but the sun was coming up. For an hour or so, Damon tried to drudge on. But his foot caught on a root and he went tumbling down into the brambles. Damon wanted to get up, and he thought about it for a moment before ultimately deciding to rest his back against a stump and sit in the mud. His injured hand ached again, but that was nothing compared to where Alejandro had grabbed him. The necrosis had spread all the way from the left half of his neck, down to his seventh or eighth rib, and halfway down his left arm. Every time his heart beat, a burning pain coursed up though the left half of his body, and the wound reeked of death. He tried peeling the dead skin from his side, but the decay was too deep, and he only wound up causing himself further damage. Sitting hurt, but walking hurt more. So, Damon sat. He cried, too. As much as he could, at least. It had been a while since he'd last done so and the feeling was almost foreign to him. Soon he was asleep.

Damon woke with the sun. Sleep had helped, but not by much. By the time the sun had rose to its zenith, he's barely made it a mile, and even then, he wasn't sure it was in the right direction. But at very least he'd at found a creek. Damon knelt at the water's edge, grass scratching at his ankles. Wincing, he lifted the shirt from off his back. Placing it at his side, he began scooping handfuls of water and letting it run down his chest. The cool water tickled into the cracks in his necrotized skin. For a moment, it felt good. But soon, the itch and burn returned.

As he continued on his way, he found himself by a ridge, where a young girl sat on a stump rubbing her head. *I went in a damn circle.* A rustle in the bushes startled him. Damon froze. From out behind a tree, he noticed barrel of a musket, and he relaxed.

"Come out Notty, it's just me."

Sean of Nottingham stepped out from behind the tree. Lowering his gun, he gave Damon a sad smile from across the way. His red capelet was ripped full up to his nape, as if it were two articles instead of one. Blood had dried all down his neck and cheek, and his clothes were covered in dirt. Damon smiled back. He stood, and began to walk across the clearing. Sara looked over at him, but there was a dazed look in her eye. About halfway across he felt a pain in his chest. *Oh god!* Damon gripped at his breast, and felt his legs give way beneath him.

The next thing he remembered was waking up next to a campfire.

Damon looked around. He was still in the forest, as far as he could tell. He groaned and raised himself to a sitting position.

"Easy."

Damon turned his head to see Brian sitting on the ground next to him, nursing what looked like a broken arm. He had a look of anguish on his face. As Damon's head became clearer, he could see a group of his friends huddled around the small fire. It was a significantly smaller group than the one he had come to shore with.

Ike stoked the fire glumly with a twig. His wing pack propped up next to him, the tips of the wooden wings singed. Next to him, Charlotte was shivering, and one of her arachnid legs was snapped and hanging limp. Nikki seemed alright physically, but the dead look in her eyes suggested another thing entirely for her mentally. She was cradling Monty; whose breathing was heavily laboured. Notty stood guard at one edge of camp, and Lionel at the other. As Brian's expression suggested: Briar was not there with them.

"We can't stay here." Damon grunted, holding his side and getting to his feet.

"And why not?" Brian glared at him. "I say we stay right here and trade *that bitch* for our people." He nodded his head over away from the fire, to where Sara was resting with her back against a tree, her chest wrapped tightly to the trunk with Charlotte's silk.

"They're alive?"

Brian shrugged. "Maybe. Maybe not. After you ran off, they got distracted. We didn't have the time to see if everyone was OK." He

gave Damon a sidelong glance. "I'm not sure whether I should thank
you for that, or curse you for leaving."

"Do whatever you need to do, but do it later," Damon told him.
"Right now, we have to get everyone to safety. They're going to be
looking for me, and even without Sara, it won't be long before one
of them picks up a trail. Brian please, we're not safe -"

"My sister isn't safe!" he snapped back. The rest of the group
stared at them. Brian had tears in his eyes. "I don't know if Briar is
alive, or dead, or... or what. But we have to go after her."

"No."

"What do you mean *no*?" Brian stood; getting face-to-face with
Damon.

Damon took a breath. Wincing, he pulled the shirt from over
his head, showing Brian the necrotic tissue riddled down his side.
He watched Brian's face soften, and heard a few gasps.

"Brian... I can't do it... and I don't think that you can either."

"I can! I'll go mysel-AHH!" He yelled as Damon grabbed his
arm.

"You can't either, Brian. We need to get to somewhere we can
rest. Recoup."

"Do you even know the way out of this forest, Damon? Because
I don't."

"We have Ike." He pulled the shirt slowly back over his head.
"He'll show us the way."

"The way to where?"

"The only safe place that we have."

* * *

When Johann opened the door, he tried to shut it as soon as he
saw who was outside, but a foot in the way stopped it from closing.

"We need help, Johann."

"Go away. You are not welcome here."

Damon pushed his way inside. "Not my biggest concern at the moment."

The rest followed him in. Johann gave Lionel a long stare as the half-beast moved past.

"They're looking for you, you know." Johann cautioned, as he locked the door.

"We know they are, Johann."

"Don't think I won't call them."

Call them? "Call who, Johann?"

"The police; they saw that fire last night. Had to put it out. Took them four hours. They're searching for whoever started it. They found a body; it was all over the news last night."

Who's body I wonder. Damon rubbed his eyes. "Look, Johann. Just... can we stay here for a few days? We'll stay out of your hair... in the basement, or even the old shed, if you haven't taken it down."

Johann looked at him for a long time. "Do I have a choice?"

"Yes. You can choose the easy way, or the hard way to do this."

Johann frowned. "The shed out back is still there. You get that. And stay away from my son and my wife."

Damon nodded, and the group made their way to the back door. On his way, Damon noticed ten euros sitting on the kitchen table. He took the money and placed it in his pocket. Johann protested, but Damon shushed him with a finger.

"You know *exactly* what this is for."

✳✳✳

Three very long days went by in that shed. No one really spoke. No one really left, other than to go to the bushes to relieve themselves, or the odd time to stretch their legs. Damon sat in a lawn chair near the dust-crusted window. A breeze wafted in through a crack and made Damon shiver. He hadn't felt warm in days. Not since Alejandro had touched him. The shed was made for country living, meaning it was quite spacious. There was room enough for them all, but not by much. Even a big shed wasn't meant to house over a half-dozen.

Damon had played here as a child, imagining it has his own little castle. *Boy, if you only knew back then...* He wondered if he'd ever get to see Grimmhaven again. A part of him hoped he would, but another part understood that he probably never would. He got up and walking to the door, stepping over Monty where he slept on the floor. He was doing better, his breathing more normal in the past day or so.

They had gotten lucky. Johann's wife Josie was a farm veterinarian. And despite their previous... encounter, she had offered them at least some help. The treatments had been a blessing, and the antibiotics and painkillers invaluable. She had set Brian's arm and slung it in a *real* cast. No more makeshift ones from Charlotte, except the one for herself. Charlotte refused for anyone to touch her broken limb. Not that it mattered, Josie had no earthly idea what to do with it. She had also helped Damon. He was now on heavy antibiotics for the necrotized tissue. Josie had also scraped as much of it off as she could. She had then wrapped him like a mummy, making Damon the most uncomfortable he had ever been. But as least he was in less pain.

It was sunny outside, and as Damon stepped out, he took a deep, dust-free breath. He spotted Johann and Josie sipping morning tea from inside the house. He waved politely, but they didn't wave back. *They want us gone. They never even wanted us here to begin with.* They wouldn't have to wait long. Damon had made up his mind. *I leave today.* He planned to go alone. *They only want me, so I'll give them me.* The suggestion would go down like a lead balloon with Brian, but he would have come to grips with it, the point was not up for negotiation. Damon was about to go back inside, when Nikki came out to join him. She was smoking on a cigarette.

"Where on earth did you get that?" Damon asked, genuinely dumfounded.

Nikki shrugged. "Found it in the shed. It's old as shit, but it still does the job."

"Where did you learn how to smoke?"

She looked at him without an expression. "It's not hard to figure out, Damon." She took another long drag.

Damon frowned, unsure how she would take the news he was about to tell her. "I'm sending the rest of you back to Grimmhaven. I want Notty to drive you all back to the Blacktooth. If you leave soon, you'll be able to make it to the beach by nightfall."

"Fine by me."

Damon shuffled his feet. "Could you tell Brian? I don't want the hassle of having to argue with him."

Nikki stomped her butt into the dirt and crushed it with her heel. "Tell him yourself." She turned without a second look and entered the shed.

Damon sighed and followed her in.

"Letting me out yet? I have to pee." Sara was still tied up, this time to an old rusty engine in a dark and dirty corner of the shed."

He sighed. "Alright, come on." He untied her. Together, he led her outside, but paused before the bushes.

"What?" she asked.

"Come with me." He turned, and pulled her along towards the house."

Sara looked at him, confused." Where –"

"Just walk."

He knocked on the door and Johann opened it. "No," the homeowner said.

"Relax Johann, all I need is your bathroom for a few minutes."

"You have five. That's it." He let them inside.

Damon led her to the bathroom and shut the door.

"I don't want you in here with me, you know. Pervert."

Damon rolled his eyes and pointed at the mirror. "We're here for *that*."

She raised an eyebrow.

Damon rolled his eyes. *This is going to sound so corny.* "Take me to your leader."

"Oh," she said. "If I do, will you let me go?"

He thought about it for a second. "Sure, but no tricks."

"No tricks," Sara agreed. She took Damon by the hand. The mirror warped and they stepped through, back into the Black Forest, inside a small run-down stone fort. Damon looked around. The design was similar to that of Grimmhaven, but far more decayed.

"Sara, you finally made it back!" Damon turned and saw Domerick walking up towards them. He was shirtless, and had a long gash across his chest. The wound looked like it had been cauterized. When he saw Damon, he frowned.

"Damn, I was hoping he'd be the one that gave me this." He traced a finger down his wound.

Sara smiled, "No, but this is the one Chris wants."

"I remember, don't worry." He noticed that Sarah's arms were tied behind her back. Wait... just who has who here?"

Damon held up a hand. "I don't want trouble."

"Too bad."

Damon could feel himself sweating. The air around him was getting hot. A bead of sweat trickled down his temple. *I didn't want to have to fight anyone.* He closed his right hand into a fist.

"Domerick, enough. I'm boiling here." The voice came from behind them.

Damon turned to see a blond-haired man, about his age, walking over to them. He was wearing jeans and button up shirt. He looked so... *normal.*

"Who are you?" Damon asked, feeling the air cool off around him. "You weren't there when everything went to shit."

The boy raised an eyebrow. "No, I wouldn't have lasted a minute before getting myself killed." He held out a hand. "I'm Christopher Andersen."

That name rings a bell. "So, you're like me?"

"I am, Mr. Grimm." He smiled. "In more ways than you know."

CHAPTER 17

amon frowned. "I've come to meet whoever it is that leads here."

"You've found him."

Christopher smiled again, but Damon didn't trust the gesture. He did not smile back. "What did you want with me?"

"Come with me and I'll show you."

He led Damon to a throne room, unlike anything that was in Grimmhaven. The throne itself was made with a fine mahogany and inlayed with gold. Christopher took a seat and smiled. The something caught Damon's eye. Something that gave him a mixture of rage and relief.

"Care to explain *that*?" He pointed to a birdcage off to one side of the throne. Inside, Theodore sat with his knees pressed up again his chest.

Chris shrugged. "Insurance, I suppose." He unlatched the cage door and opened it, grabbing Theo gently. The small man did not resist. Chris put him down on a nearby table. "But now that you're here, there's no need for it." He smiled the same sick smile. "So, did you bring it?"

Bring it? "Bring what?"

He scoffed." Um, the quill? Please tell me that you have it, or all of this would be in total vain. A big waste of time."

Damon bit his lip in contemplation as Christopher pulled a massive leather-bound book out and heaved it onto the table. It made a loud *THUMP* as dust puffed up into the air around it. Chris coughed and wafted in front of his face. "Alright, give it here."

"Why."

That perturbed him. "Because I said so." He sighed. Don't make me bring Big Bad in here."

Damon only stared.

Chris groaned "Pauly!" The huge ten-foot-tall giant that had been hurling boulders at Damon earlier in the week came lumbering sideways into the room, ducking beneath the doorframe. "Guard the door while Dom fetches Wolfy." Domerick's smile faded where he stood; apparently not liking playing the errand boy. But still, he did as he was told.

It didn't take much for Pauly to block the door. He was wider than it was, as well as taller. He need only stand there for Damon to be blocked into the room. Damon starting thinking up exit plans, just in case. There were windows, but all of them too high to climb. Otherwise, there was no other way out.

"I don't want to have to ask you again, Damon." Chris had opened the tome to a page somewhere in the back half. The paper was yellow, and cracking at the edges. *Old*. Chris made the universal gesture of *pass it here* with his hand.

"I'll give it to you. But, if you're still holding any more of my friends, I'll need them first."

"*Ugh*. Fine, fine." Chris waved his hand. "Sara, go get them from... the place." She nodded and scurried off.

Damon watched her leave. "How come they all follow you like... like you're some kind of god?"

"Because, Damon. I practically am to them. No," he corrected. "*We* are to them."

"What are you talking about?"

"This book!" He pointed excitedly. It contains all the original stories. Whatever you write in here becomes reality for them." He grinned. I can make them rich, give them power..."

"Kill them." Damon finished. "That sounds like a terrible weight to have over your head. That someone can change your destiny with the scrawl of a pen."

"You sound like everyone else who's ever came here poking their nose in my business." He frowned, but his smile returned as a few figures came in through the doorway. "Oh, there they are!"

As Pauly moved to the side, Damon could see the monkey-man leading Briar and Tyler into the throne room, Sara in tow. "There you go, now hand over the quill."

"Hold on."

Chris stamped his foot impatiently. "Hurry up!"

Damon took a few steps towards his friends, but a staff was thrown across his path.

"Wukong, enough. Let him through."

The man frowned, but moved off to the side all the same. Not speaking a word as he did. Damon moved past. Briar was looking down, a big purple bruise on her cheek. Damon lifted her chin. She had tears in her eyes, but overall seemed OK. Tyler looked more ashamed than hurt.

"Satisfied?" Chris was getting impatient.

"Give me a damn minute." Damon turned back to his friends. "Are either of you hurt?" Tyler shook his head. Briar said nothing. "Good. Take Theo and head back to the van. If you're quick, they probably haven't left yet. Go. Now."

Briar only shuffled her feet, but Tyler nodded, and picked Theo off the table. "Briar, you have to go with them. Brian is waiting for you." That made her eyes flicker. "He's worried about you."

She nodded, and then leaned in and kissed him. "Thank you," she whispered.

Damon watched as the three of them exited the room. He hoped they could find their way back, but he knew they might get lost. *It's still better than being here.*

"Happy?" Chris called. "I gave you what you wanted, now give me what I wanted."

Damon sighed, and pulled the quill from his pocket, holding it up between two fingers. "This it?"

"You tell me. It has to be original or it won't work."

Damon felt a paw snatch the quill from his hand. "Looks real to me." Wolf held it up to the light.

Chris smiled a wide grin. "Then bring it here! Let's test this baby out!" He looked around the room. "Everyone else; OUT!"

Pauly left them, as did Wukong and Sara. Damon was surprised to find he was also free to go. *He means me too.* But for some reason, he couldn't do it. Instead, he walked a few steps behind Wolf up to the throne. Chris never seemed to give him a second look, his focus fixated on the quill alone. Wolf placed it down beside the tome, and Chris wiggled his fingers before lightly picking it up. He chuckled. "Best not break another one. What should I change first?"

Wolf scoffed. "How about you fix my hand?" He held up his paw. It had gotten infected and pussy since the fight on the boat.

Chris pouted and nodded his head. "OK, lets give it a try."

Damon watched as the other boy scrawled some words down onto the page. From where he was, Damon couldn't see what it was, but what he did notice was Wolf.

"Bugger me!" shouted Wolf. The three of them stared down as his outstretched paw. The swelling began to go down, and the redness faded. Soon, all that was left was a dried ring of blood, which wolf scratched off with a nail, revealing nothing more than a small mark beneath.

"What did you write?" asked Damon.

Chris looked up and smiled at him. "I wrote: *Wolfy's hand healed instantly.*"

Damon looked at the tome unsure how he felt. "That's incredible."

Chris saw him thinking. "Don't believe it Grimm? Watch this." He began scribbling again. Damon felt a tingle inside him; a kind of twisting and warmth. He stepped back in a panic, tearing his shirt from over his head.

"What the hell did you do?!"

"I fixed what Alejandro did to you." *He has*, Damon realized. As he unwrapped his bandage, the skin beneath was perhaps a little darker and discoloured from what it had been, but otherwise it was fully healed. He stared at himself in disbelief.

The Admiral was beside himself. "I know what I want to write Andersen, give me the quill!" He reached for it, but Chris jolted his hand back and tsk-tsked.

"You know that's not how it works, Wolfy."

"Why not?" Wolf seemed angry.

"Only someone with the power can write in the book." He smiled, and presented Wolf with the quill. "Try it."

Wolf took it eagerly, and began writing in clumsy big letters. Damon waited, but nothing happened. Wolf seemed annoyed.

"What did you write?" Damon asked.

"I wrote that I had a big golden crown."

Christopher laughed. "And now watch me." He wrote the same thing that Wolf had just underneath. A golden crown appeared upon the Admiral's brow, as if made by the air itself.

"You can write anything then?" asked Damon.

"Anything, as long as it's after whatever was written last. You can't edit, just add-on to the end."

"You can write anything? Anything at all?" *No wonder generations gave their lives for this. That's too much power for any person to have.*

"Anything." Chris puzzled for a moment. "Wolfy? What was the name of that little bitch that broke all your ribs?"

Wolf was rolling his new crown in his hands, hardly paying attention. "Aghhh, I don't remember, I never caught it. The one who shot my hand though… What did you say his name was, Grimm? Tanner…? no. Tyler? It was Tyler."

"Tyler!" Chris smiled as he put quill to paper. "Tyler it is."

Damon was getting a very bad feeling. Trying to keep a level head, he asked very calmly: "What exactly are you writing?"

"Chris stopped and looked up." Oh. I'm just giving him a little bit of… poetic justice."

Damon's face dropped. He made a move to step closer, but Wolf put a newly healed paw on his chest and shook his head. Damon bit his lip, and was going to shove past. But before he could, he watched Christopher flamboyantly add a period to the end of his sentence.

"Let me see."

Chris smiled and moved to the side. "Be my guest."

Nervously, Damon moved past Wolf, and gazed over at the page. It read: *Tyler gets an arrow through the hand, and then a second one through the heart.* Damon trembled. When he looked up, he saw Christ grinning like a schoolboy. "You're a monster."

Chris' smile grew even wider. He stood with his arms out-stretched. "I am a God!"

Damon clenched his fists. But instead of punching Chris, he gave a two-handed shove to the tome. It was heavy, but slid well, and went crashing to the stone floor. Old pages flew out in a scatter as the binding came partially undone. Chris' smile wiped from his face.

"Hey!" He shoved Damon unceremoniously to the side, and knelt to collect the papers. "Wolfy, help me."

Begrudgingly, the Admiral knelt as well, and began collecting, careful not to rip the old pages in his claws. Damon looked down at the both of them, mouth twisting. He picked up Wolf's crown from where it lay on the table. With both hands, he brought it down over the beast's head, pointed end facing down. A sharp *CLANG* rang out and Wolf fell headfirst to the ground. Chris looked over in shock.

"Hey –" *CLANG!* The crown took him on the chin, and his head whiplashed around on a swivel. Damon knelt next to him, picking up the quill, and bending over the book where it lay on the floor. Chris grabbed him from behind, gripping his wrist on the hand that held the quill. "Hey! What are you doing, Grimm?!"

Damon didn't budge, resisting the weaker man as he tried to pull his hand away from the paper. He didn't speak.

Chris panicked, knowing that he wasn't strong enough. Letting Damon go, he reached over and grabbed the crown from where it lay on the floor. Reaching it, he turned back around to strike Damon down. But Damon had already finished; all he'd written were two little words on the very bottom of the very last page.

Chris dropped the crown. "What did you do!? WHAT DID YOU DO!?" He shoved Damon to one side, and Damon allowed it to happen. Chris knelt over the remains of the tome muttering "*nonononoNONONONONO*" louder and louder to himself. He tried to write something. He looked to Damon with hope in his eyes. But nothing happened. He frowned and tried again. Nothing. He kept writing, and Damon watched him. *It won't work anymore. It's over.*

Wolf stood up and rubbed his head. "What the hell just happened?"

"YOU!" Chris raised himself to his feet, practically spitting the word. His fist was gripping the quill so tightly that his knuckles had gone white. "This is *your* fault! *You* should have been protecting me!"

Wolf was still dazed, still not quite comprehending what was happening, or how mad Christopher was getting. But Damon knew. He knew exactly what was coming. But he wasn't going to intervene.

Chris moved closer, working himself up. "YOUR fault. This is YOUR FAULT!"

Wolf put up his paws. "I'm sorry Christopher, it won't happen –" Chris plunged the quill deep into Wolf's heart.

"No, nothing will happen ever again because of you!" There was fire in his eyes. Wolf collapsed to his knees, Blood trickling out from beneath the quill. Chris still held it there, not looking away.

Sara burst into the room, carrying her mirror. "Chris, we have a *huge* issue! We need to go, now! They have Dom. They have –" She saw the scene before her and stopped dead in her tracks. Chris didn't even look over at her, still watching Wolf's face as the last ounces of life exited his body, blood pooling around his shoes and soaking into the torn pages.

She looked to Damon, unsure how to react. He beckoned her closer and gently mouthed: *let him go*. She hesitated for a moment, but found herself going to the only sane face in the room. She no longer seemed to recognise Christopher.

Not a moment later, the door to the throne room was kicked open. Seven German police officers in riot gear and holding military grade firearms took positions inside. "GET ON THE GROUND, NOW!" The sergeant called out in German. Damon didn't even know if Chris *spoke* German. Whether or not he did was irrelevant, though. Chris did not move; nor did he look up. Not until a uniformed officer grabbed him from behind and wrenched his arms back and into handcuffs. Only then did he snap out of his trance. Utterly gobsmacked, he looked around, seemingly only now becoming aware of the situation. He looked with terror in his eyes to Damon. A look someone might give to say *help me*.

Damon didn't return the look. He didn't show him any sign of reassurance. He didn't smile. He didn't frown. Deadpan he spoke. "You wanted to be the King of Fantasy, Chris? Well, welcome to reality." Sara set her mirror onto the ground, and the two stepped into it.

CHAPTER 18

There was a soft *click*, and then the sound of scraping metal on stone as the cell door opened. The crewman looked up to see a stranger beckoning to him.

"Come on out now. You're free to go. Sorry about all this." The man stepped gingerly into the cell. The crewman could see now that it was Dexter. *Or was it Damon now?*

"Come on." Damon offered again. *What's wrong with this guy?* He wondered.

"What do you expect, you left him in a cage for a week after he was tied up by a giant spider girl." Nelda was behind him, giving him the what-for. She turned to the man. "Come on Arnie, it's OK."

The crewman seemed to snap out of it. Picking up his things, he began his walk upstairs.

"Arnie?" Damon mused as he unlocked the next door. "You know his name?"

Nelda frowned and put her hands on her hips. I know *all* their names.

"Who are all these people?" The voice came from behind them and made both Damon and Nelda jump.

"Sara, for the thirteenth time; in Grimmhaven, just use the doors."

She looked ashamed. "Sorry Damon, I'm still getting used to getting around" As she walked glumly up the stairs, she passed Brian as he was coming down.

"You sure that we can trust you?" He asked loudly, with Sara likely still in earshot.

Damon looked at him with a face that said: *shush, asshole.* "I like that we can. Besides, she has no one to go back to in the Black Forest."

"You think?" asked Brian. "You said Wolf was dead and Christopher captured. You don't know about any of the rest." A few of the crewmen gave each other nervous glances at the mention of Wolf's name.

I wonder how that news is going to go down. "They either were arrested like Chris, killed in a struggle, or managed to somehow hide out in the Black Forest. Besides, they only did what they did so Christopher would write down all their desires in that book. And that opportunity is gone now." He shrugged. "So, I think we're safe."

That afternoon, Damon found himself back at the small church graveyard, sitting cross-legged in front of a row of fresh stones. Normally, the graveyard was divided by family. However, Ike had made the suggestion of putting all those fought in the final battle for the Black Forest together. Everyone had seemed to like that idea. They had even moved Gruff's stone to include him. Now, it stood beside Woody's headstone. Down the line after that was Marlin's, then Tyler's, August's, Elliot's, and lastly the triplets.

"Hey."

Damon turned to see Briar walking up next to him. Her hair was down and she was carrying a bouquet of roses. "Hey."

"Mind if I join you?"

"No," he shook his head and motioned to the ground beside him. "Please."

"Thank you." She walked over and began placing a rose before each stone and said a silent prayer for each. Damon watched her silently. She paused for a noticeably longer time for Tyler's grave. When she was done, she sat down next to him. "I miss all of them," she said.

"Me too." He had hardly even known some of them, like Elliot and the triplets, but having them gone stung all the same. Damon cleared his throat and picked himself off the ground. "I should go. Lionel and Brian are waiting for me down on the beach"

Briar looked sad. "Stay a while. Please?"

Damon thought he saw a tear welling in her eye. "Ok," he conceded, sitting again. "But I can't stay long.

Briar gripped him by the arm and lay her head on his shoulder. Damon felt the fabric of his shirt begin to moisten where her cheek lay. "I don't need long."

✳ ✳ ✳

Damon, Brian, Lionel, and Theodore stood together on the shore as the crew boarded back onto the Blacktooth. As each one passed, Damon handed him a sack overflowing with gold. It was the least they could do for them and all they had been put through. Astor had been busy.

"For your troubles." Damon gave Fritz a smile as he handed him a sack weighing at least thirty pounds." He seemed content enough by it, but he never said a word of thanks. Brocksmith came up next. Damon handed him a sack. "Here you go."

Brocksmith hesitated for a moment. "Are you sure?"

Damon rolled his eyes. "I've had a lot worse done to me compared to being thrown off a navy ship." He shoved the bag into Brocksmith's arms.

Kent was next in line, the last of everyone. Damon felt a pang of guilt as he looked at the golden arm he knew was hidden beneath his thick jacket and glove. He pulled the last two sacks from the cart behind him, and piled them into Kent's arms. "For... everything."

Kent said nothing in return, and made his way up the ramp.

"All done." Lionel said, giving Damon a half-smile. Theodore was back sitting on his shoulder. "Do you think you'll be sailing back with them?"

Damon watched as steam started to billow from the stacks and frowned in consideration. Then he turned back towards Lionel and smiled. "No, I think I might stay here for a while."

- END -

To order more copies of this book, find books by other
Canadian authors, or make inquiries about publishing
your own book, contact PageMaster at:

PageMaster Publication Services Inc.
11340-120 Street, Edmonton, AB T5G 0W5
books@pagemaster.ca
780-425-9303

catalogue and e-commerce store
PageMasterPublishing.ca/Shop

CHARACTER GLOSSARY

Damon J. Grimm
Descendent of
Jacob Grimm

Christopher H. Andersen
Descendent of:
Hans Christian Andersen

Lionel La Bête
Descendent of
The Beast

Admiral Wolf Carley
Descendent of:
The Big Bad Wolf

Theodore "Theo" Thumb
Descendent of
Tom Thumb

Sean "Notty" Nottingham
Descendent of
The Sherriff of Nottingham

Brian & Briar Rose
Descendants of
Briar Rose

Piedmont "Monty" Piper
Descendent of:
The Pied Piper

Nelda Knowall
Descendent of
Dr. Know-all

Woody
Descendent of:
Pinocchio

Icarus "Ike"
Descendent of
Icarus

Headstone
Descendent of:
Solomon Grundy

Marlin
Descendent of:
Merlin the Magician

Gruff
Descendent of:
Billy Goats Gruff

Nikita "Nikki" Frost

Descendent of:
Jack Frost

Tyler Hood

Descendent of:
Robin Hood

Charlotte Webber

Descendent of:
Arachne

Astor

Descendent of:
King Midas

Zack B. Lucky

Descendent of:
Jack-be-Nimble

August Nature

Descendent of:
Mother Nature

Elliot Silverhoof

Descendent of:
Silver Hoof

Li, Hu, and Bo

Descendants of:
Ten Brothers

Dora

Descendent of:
Pandora

Sara Blood

Descendent of:
Bloody Mary

Domerick Inferno

Descendent of:
Dante

Klaus

Descendent of:
Krampus

Alejandro

Descendent of
Santa Muerte

Wukong

Descendent of:
Sun Wukong

Pauly

Descendent of:
Paul Bunyan

Davey

Descendent of:
Captain Ahab

The Dutchman

Descendent of:
The Flying Dutchman

ABOUT THE AUTHOR

Evan Chaika is an author and musician, born and raised in Edmonton, Alberta, Canada. Evan's passion for writing flourished at a young age while writing short stories with his mother. He began seriously considering writing as a career path at 20, and published his first novel at the age of 22; finding the time for writing between university coursework.

Evan's first novel; Starcharter: Protostar, is the first of its series. Its sequel is anticipated for release in late 2021 / early 2022. Evan's second novel; Grimmhaven - Secrets of the Black Forest, was released in December 2020. The Grimmhaven series is a more mythical-fantasy novel, compared to Starcharter's science-fantasy style.

Evan's writing style is mainly focused around fantasy, but he also branches out to science-fiction, horror, and even documentary. One of his main sources of inspiration is gazing at the night sky and wondering what may be found beyond, making Starcharter the natural introduction into a prosperous writing career.

Evan is extremely passionate about worldbuilding and creating magical societies; he wants to engage and encourage his readers to ponder, imagine, and theorize on what may happen in the next book. He firmly believes that half the joy of creating worlds comes from fan engagement.